For Wal

ONE

"I say, Flors, I'd get a wiggle on if I were you – the Battle-axe is on the move."

A moment later a stockinged ankle slid through the open window, and a brown brogue sought the carpeted floor of the Upper Sixth common room. The lipstick stained stub of a smouldering cigarette was flung carelessly into the rhododendrons three storeys below by a slender wrist disembodied in the gloaming, and a narrow face framed by a shock of chestnut curls suddenly emerged through the curtains.

"Lord, she's absolutely tireless," Flora complained as she scrambled in out of the cold November air. "I've lost three cigs this week because of Baxter's prowling. Thanks, Bella."

"Don't mention it," replied the sentinel, a whip-thin girl engaged in slavering butter over a crumpet freshly plucked from the toasting fork in the fire. "Catch." Abandoning the greasy knife for a moment, Bella Forsyth fished a small bottle of scent out of her embossed satchel and flung it across the room - displaying a deadly accuracy which would have rendered St. Penrith's games mistress speechless, given Bella's lacklustre performance in every P.E session she'd ever attended.

Managing to douse herself liberally in Coque d'Or before Miss Baxter descended upon them, Flora seized Pliny the Younger and arranged herself nonchalantly in a chair by the fire, one foot dangling over the arm-rest as she flicked idly through the pages of the *Epistulae*. She was a tall, loose-limbed girl with endless legs, finely sculpted cheekbones and a wide mouth which was always ready to break into a slow smile. To the younger girls of St.Penrith's there was also something distinctly mysterious in the feline curve of her hazel eyes, and many fourth formers had been moved to write odes to Flora's enigmatic beauty over the years. Indeed, not many months previously a substitute teacher newly graduated from Oxford had taken the extraordinarily bold step of quoting some fairly earthy lines from Ovid's Amores in Flora's exercise book – one assumes in a bid to woo her. Needless to say he did not last the week, and Flora remained entirely unmoved by his efforts.

"Girls," Miss Baxter boomed in stentorian accents as she burst into the room, "Miss Waverley has just informed me that an individual has been spotted hanging off the fire escape yet again, Gauloise in hand. Would any of you care to do the decent thing and accept responsibility?"

Miss Baxter – or Battle-axe to the ladies of St. Penrith's - was a robust woman of grim aspect. With her thick forearms and tight blonde bun there was definitely something of the German shot-putter about her, and her foul temper had made her deeply unpopular amongst her charges during the twelve months she'd been at the school.

"Miss Baxter," came the prompt retort from Alice Weaver, Flora's great friend, and a young lady who evinced a dangerous predilection for the anarchic, "how could *any* of us possibly source Gauloises cigarettes? I know for a fact that the post office only stocks gaspers, because my poor papa was forced to buy some when he ran out last Commem."

Miss Baxter peered down at Alice through her small pince-nez. "Thank you, Weaver, for that invaluable insight. Whilst I do not wish to dwell on the possibility of the Upper Sixth common room managing to procure such exotic fare, I should say that I do not for a moment doubt your ability to do so – particularly when the scent of Guerlain perfume still lingers in the air."

"Well played, Baxter," Bella Forsyth muttered under her breath, before taking a bite from her oozing crumpet.

"I shall give you all until breakfast to reveal the culprit," Miss Baxter announced, narrowing her eyes. "And if no one comes forward, this weekend's exeat will be cancelled as far as the Upper Sixth is concerned."

"But Miss Baxter!" wailed Olivia Fotherington-Smyth, leaping from her chair as though stung, "I simply must go home this weekend! I'm due in London for a dress fitting - it's the last one before my Presentation! I absolutely cannot be presented at court in an ill-fitting gown, Miss Baxter - I'd *die* of shame."

"Then I would suggest, Olivia," Miss Baxter replied coolly, "that you encourage the culprit to give herself up. Otherwise your dress will look as though it were off-the-peg."

This heartless pronouncement was greeted by gasps of horror and looks of unadulterated loathing; Alice Weaver, meanwhile, muttered darkly about the cruel oppression of the masses. Strangely, no looks of reproach were cast upon the eternally-popular Flora, who continued to flick through her book unperturbed, a beatific look of calm fixed upon her symmetrical features.

"Mackintosh," Miss Baxter declared, casting her beady gaze upon Flora, "come with me."

This instruction immediately elicited a chorus of anxious whispers from the common room, and, noble second that she was, Alice seriously contemplated claiming responsibility for the cigarettes in order to protect her friend. Flora quelled this incipient heroism with a quick grin, however, and, tossing the book aside, unravelled herself from the arm-chair before following Miss Baxter out of the room.

"See you at supper, ladies," she promised as she pulled the common room door closed behind her.

Flora followed Miss Baxter down the long corridor towards the staff room. The draughty halls of St Penrith's were unbearably cold in November, and the swarms of younger girls hurrying about them on their way to prep all sported the beleaguered aspect of the nearly-frozen. This was in part due to the miserliness of the headmistress and her refusal to heat the building until the girls had reached Bronte-esque levels of discomfort, and in part due to the pecuniary disadvantages of this once grand establishment. In its heyday, the gothic towers of St. Penrith's School for Girls had tended to the education of some of the most privileged young ladies in the country. Since the war, however, the student body had undergone a dramatic transformation, its numbers shrinking alarmingly, and whilst the school still catered for some of society's most well-connected offspring, their parents' ability - or willingness - to pay their fees had reached a truly dismal nadir.

Flora was a case in point. Her late father, Laszlo Medveczky, had been a Hungarian aristocrat of enormous charm, and her mother, Beatrice, one of the most celebrated debutantes of her generation. After Laszlo's death at the Battle of Jutland, however, Beatrice Medveczky (née Mackintosh) had fled back to her parent's estate in Surrey with baby Flora in tow. Flora had been packed off to boarding school as soon as she had reached the ripe old age of seven, and the whimsical Bea had contented herself with producing endless oil-paintings which now adorned the dilapidated walls of Brinkley Manor.

Occasionally Beatrice (or Bumble to her friends) was able to sell a painting to an unsuspecting relative or one of her numerous male admirers, however given the sad state of the Mackintosh coffers, this was rarely more than enough to keep the family in gin. St.Penrith's had therefore received little by way of remuneration for educating Flora for the past eleven years. Fortunately, Flora had turned out to possess an exceptional intelligence which had enabled the school to bestow a scholarship upon her at an early age. Whilst that may have appeased the headmistress, it had, alas, done little to satisfy the Bursar, who had a reputation for pursuing defaulting parents with unparalleled zeal.

"Sit down," Miss Baxter commanded as the pair reached the staff-room. "Well, I will get straight to the point, Mackintosh," she said rather brusquely, evincing a good deal of discomfort. "I am sorry to have to inform you that your uncle is dead."

"My uncle, Miss Baxter?" Flora asked sceptically, swiftly casting her mind back through eighteen years' worth of Christmases and birthdays and finding evidence of no such relation. "I don't think that I possess such a thing."

"Certainly not any longer," Miss Baxter said rather tartly, this cool response having taken her by surprise. "However, according to the missive I received from your mother earlier this afternoon, you were indeed someone's niece until two days ago."

Flora was perhaps less astonished by this revelation than many of her contemporaries would have been. Beatrice Mackintosh was possessed of what one might euphemistically call an Artistic Temperament (her own father had less charitably once described her as being noodle-brained), and although endlessly kind she had an unfortunate habit of forgetting things. Flora could recall one particular occasion on which she had returned from school for the Christmas holidays, only to discover that her mother had decided to winter abroad (apparently forgetting either that she had a child, or that Flora was due to spend the festive season with her – Flora was never entirely sure which). Finding that she had until very recently had an uncle ranked low on the list of things Beatrice had neglected to tell her over the course of her young life, and Flora accepted this with her usual sanguine good-humour.

"I wonder which side of the family he was from?" she mused aloud, much to Miss Baxter's displeasure.

"For heaven's sake, Mackintosh," she exclaimed, "I hardly think that your mother would have neglected to introduce you to her own brother."

"That just shows how little you know Beatrice, Miss Baxter," Flora replied, undeterred. "Really, I wouldn't be surprised if you were to tell me that he was my mother's twin."

"You are displaying a remarkable lack of proper feeling, Flora," Miss Baxter pronounced with awful disapproval, "it is quite Unnatural." She scowled at the school-girl through the tinted lenses of her pince-nez. Flora, with typical insouciance, simply stared back at her Housemistress with the easy good-humour which made her so popular with her contemporaries. Indeed, Flora always radiated a sense of simply taking life in her stride, and this encounter was no different: often she laughed at the world's absurdities and sometimes she commented wryly upon its failures, but she certainly never seemed anything other than utterly in control of her own destiny. A remarkable trait in one so young.

"Setting aside your lack of sensibility for one moment, Mackintosh," Miss Baxter continued, removing the spectacles and polishing them furiously with a lace handkerchief, "it is also incumbent upon me to tell you that you received a telegram not an hour ago. From Hungary."

If Miss Baxter had hoped that this intriguing development would draw some kind of reaction from her pupil then she would have been sadly disappointed, as

Flora simply smiled gently and crossed her long legs in front of her. "Well, Miss Baxter, I suppose I ought to take a look. Do you have it on you?"

Miss Baxter scowled. "I do not. It is marked as being highly private and confidential, apparently, thus persuading the post-boy that he must deliver it into your hands directly." The aptly named Battle-axe swept across to an old mahogany desk in the corner of the room, on which was perched a small brass bell. She rang it and looked expectantly at the side door to her office, which adjoined the rooms of the Deputy Housemistress, Miss Pring. She waited a moment, and rang again. Still nothing happened. "Pring!" Miss Baxter bellowed eventually, marching across to the side door and flinging it open, "bring that post-boy in here!"

A mouse-like woman in an oversized woollen cardigan scurried into the office muttering apologies, and delivered the pimply post-boy to Flora.

"Are you Flora Mackintosh?" the young man asked with evident suspicion.

"I am indeed," Flora confirmed, wishing she had another Gauloise to hand.

"Do you have any *Proof*?" the unfortunate fellow pressed, clutching a piece of paper earnestly to his chest.

"Not on me, I'm afraid," Flora replied, raising an eyebrow and effectively quelling the boy's pretensions. "Would you like to take a finger-print?"

"Of course she's Flora Mackintosh," Miss Baxter interjected impatiently. "Hand her the telegram."

In the face of such stiff female opposition the boy's resolve crumbled, and he reluctantly handed the telegram to Flora before being herded out of the room by the nervy Miss Pring.

Flora sighed before tucking it into the pocket of her navy blazer. "Thank you," she said with a sweet smile, pushing up from her chair and making to leave.

"Well, aren't you going to read it, Mackintosh?" Miss Baxter asked, blurting the question out before she could stop herself. "I have to tell you," she added with a dry laugh, "that if I had just received a telegram from Hungary then I should be most keen to discover its contents."

"And so I am, Miss Baxter," Flora replied serenely, "however I think that I shall have my supper first. It is so difficult to appreciate the epistolary arts when one is hungry, don't you agree?" And with that, Flora slipped out of the door and made her way down the long corridor back to her dormitory, leaving Miss Baxter staring after her open-mouthed.

The walls of the school were variously adorned with photographs of hearty looking girls wielding lacrosse-sticks, and notice-boards advertising such delights as Miss Pevensey's Hiking Club for Young Ladies, or Miss Waverley's ill-fated production of Hamlet (which had been intended for the end of the previous term, only to be postponed when Ophelia ran away with one of the wags from St. Penrith's for boys). Flora was just passing a poster reminding the girls not to talk to strangers (with particular emphasis lent to moustachioed men, according to the illustration), when the aforementioned Miss Pevensey bore down upon her, a pair of thick woollen socks encasing two highly-developed calves, and her suilline eyes sparkling with righteous indignation.

"Mackintosh!" she barked, demonstrating the power in those lungs which had propelled her to the top of Mt. Kinabalu the previous summer, "why, pray, are you roaming the corridors at ten minutes past six? It is high time that you were in the dining hall enjoying cook's boiled cabbage."

Miss Pevensey was on the cusp of commending to Flora the manifold benefits of this fibrous vegetable when she spied a solitary tear trickling down Flora's left cheek. "I say, Mackintosh," she blustered, "there is no need to cry. I know cabbage 'aint to everyone's taste, but dash it all…"

"It isn't the cabbage, Miss Pevensey," Flora replied with noble fortitude. "It is my poor dear uncle. He's dead, you see."

Miss Pevensey blanched at that, and sorely wished she was back at the top of a mountain. "Mackintosh," she managed to say at last, "good lord, I'm extremely sorry. If you ever.... if you should....Yes. Well, as you were." Giving Flora a bracing pat on the back, Miss Pevensey twisted her weather-beaten features into what she hoped was an expression of sympathy and swiftly hot-footed it back towards the staff-room. Flora, meanwhile, dashed the tear from her cheek and made her way onwards towards her dorm.

In Flora's defence, reader, it would be fair to say that Flora didn't enjoy manipulating her fellow man by squeezing out timely tears, or deploying the occasional devastating smile. She had been blessed with a charisma which frequently enabled her to have her own way, but she made use of these tools sparingly, and only with the intention of pursuing the path of least resistance. She was not what one would call a cynical or Machiavellian creature, and though she may not have felt remorse at having rattled Miss Pevensey, precisely, she certainly had not derived any pleasure from it.

Flora opened the door to the dormitory she shared with Alice, Bella, Pongo and Lettuce, and wandered across to the remaining chair situated by the window.

"Flors!" Alice cried in delight, "we thought she'd got you this time. Cocktail?"

Alice had, for the past two years, been romantically involved with a young man called Teddy Fortesque - former captain of rugby for St. Penrith's for Boys and general Good Egg. Teddy had recently gone up to

Oxford, yet, ever-mindful of his beloved, had made sure that he'd left Alice with a well-stocked bar before his departure. Alice had so far contrived to hide the contraband in the frame of her bed; the girls were all prepared to forgive the gentle clattering of glass whenever she rolled over in her sleep if it meant they would receive a pre-prandial drink.

"Martini, please," Flora said, tucking her feet up on the chair and settling herself cross-legged before her friends. "It wasn't anything to do with the ciggie in the end – although I'll own up in the morning, of course. Actually, it seems that an uncle of mine has just died. My ma asked the Battle-axe to let me know."

"Lord, that's frightful news, Flor," Bella said, her large brown eyes full of concern. "How did it happen?"

"No idea," Flora replied as she accepted a beaker from Alice and popped the olive between her lips. "I never met the poor fellow, so I can't say that it has been too much of a blow. Still, it *is* rather an odd feeling, I must say. One doesn't like to discover one's relations post-death – rather takes the fun out of having a family."

"Bad luck, Flors," Alice chipped in from under the bed, as she stashed the vermouth. "Will you be able to bust out of here for the funeral?"

"Lord, I hadn't thought of that," Flora confessed, making short work of her cocktail. "I received a telegram from Hungary, too, come to think of it, so perhaps that's got something to do with it."

"More than likely," chipped in Lettuce, as she popped a final olive into her mouth and stashed the cocktail shaker under her pillow. "Come on girls, we're going to be late for supper. One of the sprogs said there's treacle sponge tonight, and it would be a catastrophe to find that the Fifth form had snaffled the lot before we got there."

Flora remained curled up in her chair, and smiled up at her friends as they began to file out of the room. "I'll be down in a mo," she promised them, as she slipped her hand into the pocket of her blazer and curled her fingers around the piece of paper. "I'm just going to sit here a little longer."

"Like any company, Mack?" Alice asked gently, cocking her head to one side so that her long auburn ponytail fell across her shoulder and curled around her freckled face. "Pongo could always cover for me."

Flora smiled back at her, but shook her head. "No, you go on," said, "I'm fine, really – I shan't be long."

"Well, alright," Alice conceded. "I'll save you a seat, at any rate."

As soon as the door closed behind them, Flora drew the envelope out of her pocket and eyed it with interest. She slipped her finger under the lip and parted the gum, to reveal a small rectangular piece of yellow paper. "FLORA", it began, "IF YOU ARE READING THIS THEN IT IS CURTAINS FOR ME STOP IMPERATIVE THAT YOU COME TO SZENTENDRE AT ONCE STOP TRUST NO ONE STOP PLEASE THANK BEATRICE FOR SPLENDID PORTRAIT OF LASZLO STOP NEEDS REFRAMING STOP GOOD LUCK STOP YOUR UNCLE ANTAL."

Flora drained the dregs from her beaker and stared down at the gnomic message resting on her lap. Untimely death; a Hungarian village; a painting of her late father; and aesthetic concerns regarding framing? Flora began to feel rather regretful about never having met this uncle of hers, for anyone who could compose such an extraordinary message would no doubt have been excellent company. What, she wondered, could possibly have inspired such a peculiar summons? She hadn't visited Hungary since her father's death, and as far as she knew whatever relations she may still have there had never tried to contact her; the idea that she must now race across the channel in order to visit the family seat whilst ensuring that she "trusted no one", was therefore wonderfully intriguing.

Flora contemplated pouring herself a second martini as she made some rapid calculations. She had a small stash of money hidden in her room in the family's London apartment, and although she had no idea how she might convey herself to Hungary in practice, she was a resourceful girl and was sure that she could contrive something. In any event Flora had had quite enough of another dreary winter spent in a boarding school in the depths of Cambridgeshire, and whilst she had no doubt that a European jaunt would mean almost certain expulsion, she began to think that this fascinating telegram would almost be worth the risk.

"Oh, after all, why not?" she said aloud as she leapt from her chair in an unusual display of activity, "Carpe diem, and all that." Tucking the telegram back into her pocket and having made up her mind, Flora made her way down to the dining room to re-join her friends.

TWO

"Flora, you beast!" Alice breathed in an excited whisper, abandoning her treacle pudding and leaning over the dining table, "you must let me come with you, it sounds too thrilling for words!"

"There's no point in us both getting expelled if the whole thing turns out to be bogus," Flora replied very reasonably, eyeing the watery mound of boiled cabbage on her plate with suspicion. "It's more than likely that I'll turn up to find an empty house - but I promise I shall let you know if it turns out that there's some fun to be had."

"*Trust no one*," Alice said, her eyes glittering, "it really is too, too intriguing. What could he have meant by it all?"

"I can't begin to imagine," Flora said. "It may be that he was just something of an eccentric, but it must be worth a look. First, though, I need to get out of here. Mrs Wormesley has had the duty mistresses patrolling the grounds since Janet" – the erstwhile Ophelia – "absconded with that chap from the Boy's School, so that may be easier said than done, of course."

"Never fear, I believe I've got that covered," Alice said with a knowing nod. "I'd been planning to sneak down to Oxford in a couple of weekend's time to see Teddy," she explained, "so I've been working on an exit strategy - I'd happily lend it to you."

"That's jolly good of you," Flora replied, much struck by her chum's benevolence. "Let's discuss it further after prep. Oh lord, Miss Pevensey is watching us – look sharp."

Exercising the presence of mind which made her such a notably fine friend, Alice's hand shot across the table and seized Flora's in a demonstration of solidarity and sympathy. Flora squeezed it, before picking up a forkful of cabbage and surveying it woefully. Much struck by this display of tenderness Miss Pevensey directed her attentions to her supper, attacking a bowlful of treacle sponge and custard with furious energy.

After a particularly gruelling evening throughout which Miss Baxter patrolled the house with matchless zeal, the girls didn't have a chance to resume the topic of Flora's imminent escape until they found one another, toothbrushes in hand, at adjacent basins shortly before lights out.

"I say, Flora," Alice said through a mouthful of foam and bristles, "have you packed? You must take something from the bar for the journey – Lord knows what they drink in Hungary."

"Some kind of fruit brandy, I believe," Flora replied, rubbing at her flawless face with a light-blue flannel. "Mother has it shipped from Budapest in her more extravagant moods. That's very kind of you, though – I must say, it would be nice to have an emergency stash."

"That's the spirit," Alice said encouragingly. "I'll lend you my hip-flask."

When they once again returned to their dormitory, Olivia positioned herself as look-out whilst Alice decanted some Oban whisky into a very pretty silver hip-flask. Flora, meanwhile, exchanged her flannel pajamas for a red cable-knit sweater and a pair of tan slacks.

"I can't believe you're running away, Flora," Pongo said, positively fizzing with excitement. "I say, I'd be *terribly* honoured if you would take my lucky scarf to see you on your way." Pongo rooted around in the trunk at the foot of her bed for a minute before emerging triumphant with a streak of blue cashmere, which she gave to her friend in the reverent manner of one making a votive offering.

"Lord, Pongo," Flora said, the soft fabric between her fingers, "are you quite sure? This is terribly generous of you."

"Oh, it's nothing," Pongo said with a dismissive flick of the head, her cheeks flushed with pleasure, "it's the very least I can do in the face of such pluck. You can give it back to me at Bella's Christmas Party."

"Right, we ought to make a move," Alice announced, tucking the hip-flask into Flora's small shoulder bag and guiding her friend towards the door. "Say your farewells, girls."

Flora embraced each of her cohorts before flashing a bright smile and following Alice out of the door. "See you soon, ladies – wish me luck."

"*Good luck!*" they cheered in unison as loudly as they dared; "Break a leg, Flors!" Flora heard Lettuce - a budding thespian – cry, as the door closed behind her.

"Follow me," Alice whispered, plastering herself against the wall and edging cautiously down the corridor in the manner of a master-criminal. Flora followed suit, sticking to the shadows and holding her breath whenever she heard a sound. In this way they crept down three flights of stairs, past the dorm rooms and into the belly of the school.

"I feel rather like Arthur J Raffles," Alice whispered as they passed down a final flight of stairs and into the school's utility rooms, "sneaking about like this. Absolutely *thrilling*."

At last they stopped in a dark, damp corridor leading from the kitchens to the gardeners' store-room, and Alice pulled a small torch from the pocket of her dressing-gown. Pausing a moment to ensure that they really were alone, Alice flicked the switch and bathed the stone floor in a ray of weak, yellow light.

"This is the plan," she said in a soft voice, spinning the torch around to illuminate her freckled face. "One of the junior gardeners keeps a spare pair of overalls in that cupboard. You'll put them on, pull this cheese-cutter over your eyes," Alice drew a tweed hat from the depths of her other pocket, "and push the wheel-barrow in the corner there over to the door by the kitchen-garden. It's never locked between nine and midnight on a Thursday evening, because Miss Chatterley sneaks out to play darts at The Dog and Whistle. If anyone should see you, they'll assume you've just been working late on the cabbages. Any questions?"

Flora pulled the flat-cap onto her head and tucked a cigarette behind her ear. "Top-drawer strategising, Alice," she said appreciatively, as her friend handed her the muddy overalls. "Very comprehensive. How did you discover Miss Chatterley's mania for darts, out of interest?"

"Teddy's younger brother creeps out of school to play for the same team using an assumed name, so I've been on to her for a while now."

"I see," Flora replied, accepting the reasonableness of this explanation at once. She pulled herself gingerly into the overalls whilst Alice hopped about from one foot to the other in a bid to stay warm. "Well, Ali, this is it," Flora said as she threw her shoulder-bag into the wheelbarrow. "Thanks ever-so for letting me use your disguise, you really are a rock."

"Don't mention it, darling," Alice replied, ignoring the dirt which now covered her friend's torso and pulling her into a firm hug. "Be safe – and for heaven's sake let me know how you get on, I shall be absolutely desperate with curiosity."

And with that Flora disappeared into the night, pushing her creaky wheelbarrow towards liberation and adventure. She was indeed spotted by Mrs Wormesley's

Cerberus for the evening (a timid mathematics mistress called Miss Twee), and if Miss Twee had been less myopic, she may have noticed there was something rather unusual about the way the gardener was hurrying down the path. As it was Flora made it to the door unimpeded, and soon found herself standing in the middle of a pitch-dark country lane on a moonless night not three miles from Saffron Waldon. It occurred to her, as she peeled herself out of the overalls and flung them back over the wall, that she hadn't really considered what her next move might be once she'd escaped from St.Penrith's. She knew she'd need to stop off at the Mackintosh residence in London, but how to get from Sewards End to Knightsbridge posed something of a challenge. Unperturbed, she took a small sip from the hip-flask (Alice would no doubt have been gratified to know that her gift had come into its own less than two metres from the school boundary) and set off in the direction of Cambridge; the twenty miles would require a full night's walking of course, but there it was – Flora could be athletic when the mood took her so she set off at a fair pace, thankful for the sturdiness of her highly polished brogues.

As she walked through the rosy twilight Flora admired the unabashed flatness of the county's topography, as she had often done before. There was something about the land's refusal to carve itself into showy peaks and lyrical valleys that appealed to her sense of practicality; it may not inspire any Wordsworthian nods to the mountain's echo but this very English scene was quietly beautiful in its own way.

Just as Flora was giving herself up to these contented meditations, she became aware of a pair of bright lights bowling along behind her and she scrambled up onto the bank, ready to flag the driver down. She'd barely managed to vacate the road when the vehicle hurtled towards her; using the burning embers of her cigarette as a makeshift distress flare she waved her arms in the air and called for assistance. Flora heard the screech of tyres and, much relieved, smelt the tell-tale stench of burnt rubber as the car juddered to a halt a few yards ahead of her.

"Hell's teeth!" a furious male voice shouted, "what the dickens are you doing in the middle of a country lane at this time of night? I could very easily have killed you - which really would have capped off what has already been an atrocious day, let me tell you."

"I'm awfully sorry," Flora said at her most charming, "you appeared so unexpectedly, you see."

Flora had by this time stepped into the pool of light being cast by the headlights of the bright red MG, and the driver, who had clearly been winding himself up to launch into a diatribe against idiotic hikers, was brought up short.

"Well," he said gruffly as he observed this unexpected oasis of beauty adrift in the sticks, "no harm done, I suppose."

"None whatsoever," she reassured him with a winning smile, "I'm quite alright."

The man, who appeared to Flora to be in his mid-thirties and possessed of a pleasantly ruddy face, was sporting a thick tweed suit, a woollen scarf in the colours of one of the Cambridge colleges, and a mop of dark hair which the car's backdraught had left in disarray. She noted also that other than appearing to be slightly harassed, he seemed perfectly agreeable – the sort of fellow a girl could trust in a crisis.

"I wonder, Mr....?"

"Moore," the man replied after only the slightest hesitation, leaping out of the car to offer the young lady his hand, "Professor William Moore."

"Well, then, Professor Moore," Flora said, correcting herself with a smile, "I wonder whether you might be heading in the direction of Cambridge?"

The gentleman looked a shade taken aback by this, and shuffled from one foot to the other whilst fishing in his pockets for a cigarette. "Er....." he replied vaguely, his search apparently proving to be unsuccessful.

"Allow me," Flora said, offering Professor Moore one of the Gauloises from her bag.

"I say, thanks very much," he replied appreciatively, lighting the cigarette and leaning back against the door of his car. "As a matter of fact, I'm making for London," he replied, the soothing effects of the French nicotine rendering him far less fidgety. "Matters of business, you know," he added vaguely.

"Well, that's famous!" Flora cried in delight, as she moved towards the passenger door with decided intent. "How would you feel about having a passenger?" Flora turned the beam of her melting blue eyes upon him, and offered up a smile which managed to convey just the right amount of helplessness blended with a quiet sort of courage.

Professor Moore attempted to smooth the unruly hair at his crown and puffed meditatively on the cigarette. "Why not," he announced at last, leaping back into the car and opening the passenger door for Flora. "Climb aboard."

Needing no further encouragement, Flora clambered into the small MG and, somewhat prematurely, thanked her lucky stars as Professor Moore put the vehicle into gear and set off at speed.

"So," he asked, as they rounded yet another hair-pin corner in fourth, "what the devil are you doing out here at this time of night? I say," he added, the spark of inspiration in his eyes, "are you a teacher at that girls' school? On the lam from the staff room, as it were?"

Flora, who was finding it jolly difficult not to yelp in horror every time Professor Moore approached another bend in this impossibly winding road, clung on to her seat and replied with as much calm as she could muster, "Sixth former, not teacher. And not running away, as such – just slipping off for a few days to take care of some family business." She was struggling to hear anything above the roar of the straining engine, however Flora was fairly certain that Professor Moore had groaned at the mention of families. Pulling the hip-flask from her bag, she took another sip of Oban whisky in a bid to fend off both the cold and the terror evoked by his extraordinarily erratic driving, and wrapped Pongo's scarf around her head to preserve her curls.

"What was it about your day that was so atrocious?" she asked, recalling the comment he had made shortly after screeching to a stop. "I don't suppose it had anything to do with your driving?"

"In a manner of speaking, it did, actually," he conceded, shaking his head in an attempt to rid himself of the memory. "Absolutely shame-making - I really don't know how I'll show my face in college next week."

"What in heaven's name did you do?" Flora asked in gentle amusement, the whisky beginning to give her a pleasant inner glow, "You didn't kill anyone, I hope?"

"Only my career," he replied glumly, tossing the stub of his cigarette into the night and wishing he had another to hand. "I was taking my Aunt Muriel for a punt, you see," he began, bellowing above the noise of the engine, "and I rather lost my bearings."

"What happened?" Flora shouted, reading her chauffeur's mind and offering him another timely Gauloises.

Professor Moore sighed and, after a struggle, managed to light his cigarette. "The BBC had picked today of all days to film the Blues in training, ahead of the Boat Race in April," he replied unhappily. "And I....well, I managed to push our blasted punt into a direct collision course with their boat. The cox tumbled in headfirst, and half dragged Aunt Muriel with him. The whole thing was caught on celluloid, of course, and the Master of Magdalene was looking on too - which will do my already-precarious position in College no good whatsoever." He puffed forlornly on his cigarette. "I've just taken a sodden Aunt Muriel home – having spent the remainder of my afternoon listening to a lengthy tirade about how she's now determined to write me out of her will, and instead leave everything to my loathsome cousin Eustace. So yes, it's been something of a stinker."

Flora threw her head back and gave herself up to whoops of laughter. "How marvellous," she said, gasping, "I wonder whether they'll air it? I *do* hope so."

Professor Moore, his dark hair blowing all over the place, glanced resentfully at her before assuming a piously pained expression. "I consider it distinctly heartless of you to laugh at my misfortune. I have had a most uncomfortable day."

"Don't be so poor-spirited," Flora replied with a chuckle. "I am sure that your Aunt will forgive you in time to disappoint Eustace, and imagine how popular you shall be if the footage does go out – it sounds just like something out of a Charlie Chaplin picture."

Professor Moore's demeanour softened slightly, and he permitted himself a rueful smile. "Well, I must say that it has been a relief to share the horror with somebody – and I daresay it was rather amusing for the spectators. I shall be in no end of trouble with my mother, tomorrow, though. Lord, what a lowering thought."

One of Flora's numerous advantages was the fact that she was not, by nature, an introspective girl. Many young ladies in her circumstances would have been wracked by nerves, endlessly turning over in their minds the fact that they were charging into the unknown; that they had no idea what they might be walking into in Szentendre; and that the telegram from the self-styled Uncle Antal had contained the distinct suggestion of Foul Play. As it was, Flora was able to make herself quite at home in the little MG, proffering the occasional observation but otherwise enjoying her whisky and the exquisite stillness of the winter's evening. Professor Moore was also privately delighted to have the company – the one ray of sunshine in an otherwise ghastly day - and by the time they arrived on the outskirts of London, they were both very pleased with one another.

"Where would you like me to drop you?" Professor Moore asked, as they sped past Alexandra Palace. "I'm heading to Hampstead myself, but I'd be delighted to take you wherever you need to go."

"That's awfully good of you," Flora replied, thanking the fates once again for steering this delightfully eccentric man in her direction, "I'm heading for Mayfair actually, but that's a good distance out of your way."

"Nonsense," Professor Moore replied, brimming with sudden gallantry, "I'm in no particular hurry, and must see you safely to your destination before heading home to face the music, as it were."

He would brook no argument, and so it was that rather than having to make her own solitary nocturnal journey from Cambridgeshire to the city, Flora found herself deposited at the steps to the Mackintosh's apartment block by her new friend.

"You're such a terrific sport," she said as she leapt from the vehicle, offering the Professor a final cigarette as a parting gift. "Thank you."

"Don't mention it," Professor Moore replied gaily, greatly restored by his time in the company of this charming young woman. "Do look me up when you are next in Cambridge – I should very much like to take you to tea at the Orchard, if you'd be brave enough to get into a punt with me." Revving the engine in a final display of renewed exuberance, the Professor put the MG into gear and sped off down the road at a truly reckless speed.

Flora watched him go and then, rummaging through her bag, fished the keys out, nodded to the night porter and walked up the two flights of stairs to her mother's apartment.

THREE

It was almost eleven by the time she walked into the dark hallway, and Flora was decidedly ready for her bed. She kicked off the brogues, unwound the scarf from her head and shook out her curls before heading towards the living room to pour herself a quick night-cap. She flicked the light on in the hallway as she moved through the apartment, eyed her mother's curious taste in bronze statuettes with misgiving (all of which had apparently frozen with embarrassment at various stages of the dance of the seven veils), and dangled a cigarette between her scarlet lips. Suddenly she stopped, lighter held motionless in mid-air. The muted strains of Duke Ellington's "In a Sentimental Mood" wafted towards her from the crack under the living room door, and she could just make out what appeared to be lamp-light spilling from the room.

Her mother was supposed to be in Paris attending a series of life-drawing classes and, although Flora was only too aware that where Beatrice was concerned such plans meant very little, she decided it would be best not to take any chances - particularly given the ominous undertones in her uncle's telegram. Seizing one of the statuettes, Flora crept towards the doorway. The bronze dancer, Flora was pleased to note, had managed to retain a single swathe of thin material about her pneumatic person; Alice might enjoy the anarchic possibilities of beating an intruder over the head with a bare bronze bosom, but the idea struck Flora as being rather vulgar.

Pushing the door open Flora edged into the room, Gauloise in mouth, statuette in hand, and eyes narrowed in suspicion.

"Darling one!" her mother squealed, nearly overturning her easel as she jumped up to embrace her daughter, "I had no idea you were in Town!"

Flora had to hand it to Beatrice; she certainly knew how to create a spectacular tableau. The burgundy walls were positively glowing with the amber light being cast by numerous candelabra, and the fire was blazing with such intensity that the room felt almost tropical. Beatrice had created an artistic haven for herself by the far window; her easel was surrounded by velvet throws, plump cushions were strewn about its legs like small, sleeping animals, and Flora was sure that she could spy a bottle of Veuve-Clicquot tucked away by the paintbrushes. The real surprise, however, came in the form of a naked man standing in the middle of the room, his modesty protected only by a bunch of artfully placed grapes. Beatrice's portrait suggested that he ought to have been evincing a kind of languid, classical sprezzatura; as it was, he looked distinctly uncomfortable and inescapably English.

Beatrice flung her arms around her only child, encasing Flora in that familiar smell of turps, Vol de Nuit and tobacco. She was still an extraordinarily beautiful creature possessed of a poker-straight blonde bob, china-doll eyes and a slender figure which belied her maternal status. Unless one knew better, one might assume that the two women were sisters.

"Hallo, Beatrice," Flora said, passively accepting this embrace and extending her arms so that her mother would neither be stabbed by the flailing limbs of the bronze dancer nor set alight by her cigarette, "I thought you were in Paris."

"I *do* wish you'd call me mother, dearest," Beatrice replied, sighing theatrically and wafting back across the room to retrieve her champagne. "I'm not sure it's terribly appropriate of you to be bandying my name about like that, even if it does make me feel considerably younger than "mama" would. Anyway, I *am* in Paris. I only popped back for the day to run a few errands – you know – when I bumped into Teddy here. One simply had to immortalise him in oil. He has such an exquisite jawline, it would have been criminal of me to leave him in Harrods."

"Yes," Flora said slowly, "how silly of me not to notice his inspirational jaw."

"I'm Bertie Cavendish," the young man interjected, seizing a dressing gown from the sofa behind him and managing to wriggle into it without mishap. "It's a pleasure to meet you."

Now that she was no longer distracted by his marble flesh, Flora was at liberty to observe that her mother's muse was in fact a very handsome young man. He was tall, athletically built, and smiling at her in the most charmingly crooked way. She guessed that he must be in his mid-twenties and, from the unmistakeably intelligent look in those hazel eyes, not your run-of-the-mill nudist.

"Flora Mackintosh," Flora replied with a slight incline of the head, as she accepted a saucer of champagne from her mother and arranged herself on a chaise-longue near the mahogany drinks cabinet.

"Now, darling," Beatrice said, sweeping across the room in the long black velvet jacket she always wore when she was painting, "shouldn't you be in school?"

"Indeed I should, Beatrice," Flora replied, unperturbed, "however I've received a most unexpected telegram from a man claiming to be my uncle, and it looks as though I shall have to go to Hungary."

"Good lord, Antal!" Beatrice said with a gasp, clapping a milky-white hand over her pretty mouth, "do you know, I have been *so* distracted by Bertie that I utterly forgot about him. How absolutely ghastly of me."

"I say, would it be better if I waited in the other room?" Bertie asked, knotting the dressing gown cord and edging towards the door. "Give you both a little privacy?"

"Oh no, Bertie darling," Beatrice said, wafting her hand rather vaguely. "He wasn't a close relation. Have a little more champagne."

"Close or not, you might have told me that I had an uncle," Flora observed, remonstrating gently. "It was quite a blow to receive a telegram from him and to hear the news of his death on the same day. Miss Baxter was agog with curiosity."

"Who is Miss Baxter?" Beatrice asked vaguely. "Is she a friend of yours, my love?"

"She is my Housemistress," Flora replied simply, deciding not to reveal to her mother that she and Miss Baxter had met above ten times, and had even sat next to one another during the speeches at Commem the previous summer. "Uncle Antal said thank you for the portrait of Father, by the way. He described it as being "splendid"."

"Did he?" Beatrice replied, evidently slightly confused. "How very peculiar of him. I'm terribly glad he liked it, of course, but I've only ever given him one picture and I'm sure that that was more than twenty years ago. I'm no stickler for punctuality, of course, but two decades seems an indecently long time to wait to send a thank you note."

Flora did not hold much store by this. If Beatrice could forget that she had a child for huge swathes of the year then she could certainly send a painting to Hungary without remembering she'd done so. It did seem rather odd, but Flora didn't consider it to be something worth dwelling on; if Uncle Antal's powers of recall and punctuality were anything like her mother's, then it seemed perfectly possible that his thank you note could indeed have been so tardy.

"Now how long are you staying, my own one?" Beatrice asked as she placed a Lucky Strike in the tip of her amber cigarette holder. "I thought that I might head back to Paris in a day or so – you'd be more than welcome to join me. There's plenty of room in the pension, and it's always such a scream in Montmartre."

"That's terribly kind of you, Beatrice," Flora replied, genuinely touched by this unusually expansive maternal gesture, "however I really must be setting off for Budapest in the morning. Uncle Antal was quite specific regarding the level of urgency required, and in any case if I don't get a move on the school is sure to catch up with me."

"I quite understand, my love," Beatrice replied abstractedly as she started to dab at the portrait of Bertie with a fine brush. "How are you planning to get there?"

Flora dipped her nose into the champagne saucer. "As a matter of fact I hadn't made any firm decisions on that front," she confessed. "What would you recommend?"

"If I may," Bertie interjected, taking a seat opposite Beatrice and absent-mindedly eating the grapes, "I think I may have just the thing."

"Really, Bertie?" Beatrice exclaimed, entirely charmed by this pronouncement. Flora waited in measured anticipation.

"Well, I'm something of an amateur pilot, you see," he said somewhat bashfully. "Ma and Pa gave me a light air-craft last Christmas, and I'm always jolly keen to use it any chance I get. In short," he added, throwing a grape high into the air and catching it in his open mouth, "I should be delighted to run you across to Hungary tomorrow, if you like."

"What is it that you say you for a living, Mr Cavendish?" Flora asked, reluctantly impressed by this surprising offer of aerial transportation.

"I didn't," he replied with a grin. "Currently, Miss Mackintosh, I would say that I am a flâneur."

"How desperately romantic," a delighted Beatrice replied, clapping her hands once again. "Why, I am half minded to go with you myself!"

"Alas, it is only a two-seater," Bertie replied, quashing this fledgling dream. "However I should be more than happy to fly you anywhere you wish once I have returned from dropping Flora off."

Flora lit a cigarette and puffed on it thoughtfully. Her uncle had told her not to trust anyone, of course; however, she didn't for one moment imagine he would include the nude, grape-throwing Bertie in his camp of suspicious characters. The fellow may be a touch *unusual*, but he certainly didn't scream danger. Moreover it seemed to present the perfect solution to her problem. She'd seen advertisements for the new night ferry between London Victoria and Gare du Nord in *The Times* (which she had delivered to St.Penrith's each day, and typically enjoyed reading whilst drinking her first cocktail of the evening) but even were she to experiment with a channel crossing, she'd still need to find a car in France and navigate her away across the continent. In short, Bertie's offer was extremely tempting, and she was minded to accept it.

"I can of course procure character references, should you wish to have some comfort on that score," Bertie offered magnanimously, as Beatrice topped up his glass. "Wilky and Jumbo are more than likely to be making inroads into the Travellers Club's single malts at this sort of time, and I'm sure they would be more than happy to vouch for me, if we called them up."

"I don't suppose that will be necessary," Flora replied graciously, finishing her champagne and rising from the chaise-longue. "If you're quite sure that it wouldn't be an imposition then I should be most grateful for your assistance, Mr Cavendish. Shall we start after breakfast? Say 11 o'clock?"

"Splendid," a beaming Bertie replied, genuinely pleased to have had his offer accepted. "I should be making tracks myself in that case – lots to be done before the morning."

"Oh, but I haven't finished your portrait!" Beatrice cried in dismay, "and it has been coming on so promisingly. It would be very naughty of you to leave." Beatrice's bottom lip threatened to quiver, and those limpid blue eyes glistened with un-spilled tears.

"Never fear," Bertie replied kindly, "we shall finish it before too long, and I must say that you are doing such a top-rate job – I've never looked so regal."

Beatrice beamed with pleasure, while Flora studied this thoughtful and most peculiar young man with decided interest.

FOUR

The next morning, Flora trotted down the stone steps to the street below, sporting a very smart pair of high-waisted charcoal trousers, a matching grey beret and a guernsey-sweater in racing green. Pongo's scarf was draped carelessly about her shoulders, and she carried a light travelling case in one hand and a small handbag in the other, the latter filled with all the essentials she suspected she may require during her time in Hungary: cigarettes; Alice's hip-flask; a tube of red-lipstick and a pistol.

In a display of uncharacteristic punctuality, Bertie was waiting by the pavement in a very smart Aston Martin Le Mans. As soon as he saw her, he tooted the horn in greeting.

"Morning!" he cried. "Sleep well?"

"Beautifully, thank you," Flora replied, bestowing a grateful smile upon him. "One never sleeps so well as one does in one's own bed, does one?"

"One does not," Bertie replied in solemn agreement, as he took Flora's suitcase from her and stowed it in the boot. "I hope you were given a good feed, too," he added. "I'm afraid that we'll be in the air for the best part of the afternoon, and there's only room for the most rudimentary of picnics in Cynthia-Rose."

"Who, or what, is Cynthia-Rose?" Flora asked, much amused by this warning.

"Ah," Bertie said, firing up the engine and speeding off in the direction of Wimbledon Common. "Cynthia was my maternal grandmother, you see, and Rose my paternal. They were wonderful women and both lived to a very great age, so I thought it would be rather a promising omen to name my little plane after them. So far, so good."

Flora laughed and glanced across at her companion as he navigated his way through the busy London streets. There was something about him that she couldn't quite place. He looked for all the world like the carefree young man he claimed to be and there was no doubt that he was exceedingly charming, but there was something that didn't ring entirely true to her, somehow. A keen intelligence lurked in those eyes of his, and a decided air of mystery. She didn't feel unsafe in any way, but she resolved to keep an eye on this convenient knight-errant.

"She's parked over in Wimbledon," he explained, "so we should be up amongst the clouds in no time."

Flora drew a cigarette from her bag, and popped it between her lips. "So what did you do before you were flâneuring, Mr Cavendish?" Flora asked, blowing smoke up into the frosty morning air. "I can't believe that you've spent a great deal of time modelling for women you've encountered in Harrods. Which section, by the way?"

"Food hall," Bertie replied, taking his eyes off the road for a moment to look across at her. "They stock a particular kind of stilton that I've so been unable to find anywhere else, and which I find I cannot live without."

"How romantic," Flora retorted with the ghost of a smile. "Their eyes met across a crowded fish counter."

"It was by the eggs, actually," Bertie replied, unfazed by this sally. "However I can assure you that there was nothing of *that* kind going on, Miss Mackintosh – my afternoon with your mother was spent solely in the pursuit of art. She really is very talented, you know."

"I know," Flora said simply. "She paints beautifully."

"To answer your question, though," Bertie said, skilfully weaving his way through the streets of South London, "I have had several professions. I was in the Royal Navy for a time; after that I spent a year or so working on a vineyard in France; and then there was a brief spell in Nairobi. I've been back in London for about twelve months now, and I must say that I was beginning to get rather restless again. This jaunt across the channel couldn't have come at a better time, let me tell you."

Bertie suddenly swung the car down a small, wooded lane on the outskirts of Wimbledon, drove through a wide gate and killed the engine. "She should be perfectly safe here for today," he reassured Flora, as he leapt out of the car and moved around to open her door. "Come along."

The pair gathered their things and left the car nestled behind a hawthorn hedge. Bertie strode off towards the common at a yomping pace. "She's just over here," he called over his shoulder. Flora crossed the road and strolled after him, enjoying the feeling of the bright winter sunshine on her skin and the pleasant anticipation of adventure. A cluster of children were trying to fly a kite in the distance, and the treeless green plain stretched out before her; the perfect runway she thought to herself, ever the pragmatist. Flora watched Bertie as he marched across the still-frozen soil, and quietly pondered the new facts she had gleaned during their drive. The revelation about the Navy immediately made sense to her – his particular brand of restless energy tallied with her notion of a former serviceman looking for excitement. It also justified her instinctive sense of faith in him; her father had served in the High Seas Fleet after all, and as far as she was concerned there was nothing as trustworthy as a sailor.

Bestirring herself from this quiet reflection, Flora's eyes widened as Bertie swept away a sheet of green tarpaulin to reveal a bright red, single-engine aeroplane. She didn't know quite how it could have taken her so long to spy the bulge in the middle of this open expanse and yet there it was, with "Cynthia-Rose I" emblazoned along its side in swirling black letters. *"What sort of a fellow leaves a plane on Wimbledon Common?"* she thought to herself in astonishment. *"One wonders what he's got stashed in Hyde Park."*

"Here she is," Bertie said proudly, stroking one of her curved wings with affection and dropping to his haunches to inspect the underbelly. "Isn't she a beauty?"

Flora was moved to agree with this statement, and walked towards the pretty aircraft with a distinct spring in her step, as her shock gradually abated. "I say – this beats the night ferry."

"Rather," Bertie agreed whole-heartedly, stowing the small suitcase and hamper in the seat to the rear and leaping up into his pilot's seat to make ready for take-off. As he fiddled with the assortment of dials and buttons, Flora pulled a leather flying cap out of her bag, a pair of tan leather gloves and a large pair of goggles: Beatrice had collected a remarkable array of paraphernalia during her endless travelling, and Flora had found these particularly useful items when rummaging through the camphor wood chest in the hall earlier that morning (shortly before she had been guided forcefully towards a large plateful of kedgeree by her mother's faithful housekeeper).

"Well, don't you look the thing!" Bertie exclaimed with an appreciative laugh, as Flora donned her accessories and hauled herself up into the passenger seat. "Are you quite sure you haven't done this before, Flora? You seem remarkably well prepared."

"I like to be prepared in all things, Bertie," Flora replied, peering at him through her goggles and arranging her chestnut curls around the edges of her cap. "Could there be anything worse than being stranded on a station without a book? Or to find oneself with stacks of tonic and no gin? No - the readiness is all," she announced with resolution.

"I'm not entirely sure that that's the accepted scholarship regarding the Bard's immortal words," Bertie ventured, pulling a neat little hip-flask from the pocket of his leather jacket, "but I think you may be on to something." He offered the flask to Flora, who brought it to her nose for identification.

"Bruichladdich," she said appreciatively, the familiar smell warming her to her toes. (Teddy Fortesque may have been on course to fail Collections, but at least he could take pride in the first class training he had imparted to Alice and her friends through his exquisite contraband.)

"You have an excellent nose," Bertie replied, much impressed. "I never fly without offering a libation to the gods first," he added, gesturing to the skies with his own gloved hand. Flora was entirely in sympathy with this sentiment, and the pair toasted their imminent journey with a moment's solemnity before Bertie returned the hip-flask to his pocket and flicked the switch for the engine.

Jumping down from the small plane and then with a strong sweep of his arm, Bertie spun the propeller and brought Cynthia-Rose to life; the aircraft juddered as she cleared her pipes and prepared for flight. Bertie hauled himself back into his seat, gave Flora the thumbs up, and drove inexorably towards the kite-flyers. After two hundred yards of coasting across the uneven grass Cynthia-Rose launched herself into the air, swooping above the delighted children and sending their kite swirling upwards in the backdraught. Flora, who despite her pertinent accessorising had never been in an aircraft before, looked around her in wonder. The people below them grew smaller as they climbed, and the shrubby grass on Wimbledon Common turned into a table-cloth spread across the southern corner of the city. The cold air stung her cheeks and made Pongo's scarf dance about her neck, and Flora felt her stomach fizz with delight every time she was brave enough to stare down over the side. It was a clear day, cold and bright, and it felt like no time before they were over open country.

Bertie looked back and, through a series of elaborate hand gestures, managed to ask Flora to open the hamper. Reaching down to the wicker case by her feet she undid the clasp and lifted the lid, only to be greeted by a bottle of Champagne De Castelnau, two glasses and a large pork-pie. If she had been her mother, she might have clapped her hands in delight. As it was she smiled brightly up at her pilot, popped the cork from the bottle and, after some extremely careful pouring, managed to hand him a frothing glass of wine.

"Delicious!" she shouted as loudly as she could into his ear. This was, she thought to herself contentedly, considerably better than double Latin.

Bertie knocked back the first glass of fizz and handed it back to his passenger for a refresher. "Have you been to Hungary before?" he shouted, that deep English voice rising above the wind.

"I was born there," Flora managed to tell him through a combination of careful annunciation and cradling an imaginary infant. "But I haven't been back for many years. Not since my father died."

Bertie nodded in understanding, and glanced back at the nose of the plane to check that they were still flying in the right sort of direction. Flora carved off a hunk of pork pie (heaven to discover the eggs nestled in its core, she thought) and passed it forwards. It was either excessively comforting or rather alarming to think that this young man was happy to fly towards France with a glass in one hand and a slice of meat pie in the other, leaving his knees to do any steering - but he seemed to know what he was doing, and the clouds were passing them at a serene pace. She was also fairly sure she hadn't seen him stow any parachutes, she realised as she refilled her own glass; however if Bruichladdich wasn't enough to appease the heavens then what, she wondered, at her most existential, was the point of it all.

"Je veux que la mort me trouve plantant mes choux!" she cried out to the clouds before taking a large sip from her glass and slipping a portion of hard-boiled egg into her mouth.

Bertie thought that he could hear his cargo saying something about cabbages, and toasted the strange sentiment with an unimpeachable sense of fun.

The English Channel slipped away beneath them, and Flora leant back in her seat and gazed up at the sky. Apart from the sound of the engine, the world was completely still: no voices; no bells governing each portion of her day; no clashing hockey-sticks or bellowing mistresses. Absolute bliss.

"We're making good time," Bertie shouted over his shoulder after adjusting their course slightly, "we should be there while it's still light."

Flora half-wondered what Bertie intended to do once they'd landed; she didn't suppose that she would be able to offer much by way of hospitality, and she certainly hadn't planned on having a plus one during her investigations into her uncle's death. Still, he didn't seem like a clinging sort of fellow, and although she couldn't remember the dimensions of the family seat she imagined that it must at least have a stray sofa the poor man could sleep on for the night.

Idly helping herself to another glass of champagne, it suddenly occurred to her that he hadn't consulted a map or a compass for the duration of their journey. If Beatrice's romantic descriptions were anything to go by then Szentendre was hardly what one would call a backwater, however it struck her as rather peculiar that a flâneur should have such a sound grasp of Eastern

European geography. Not for the first time, Flora suspected that there was far more to Bertie Cavendish than he was letting on.

"I say, Bertie," Flora began, leaning forwards to speak in his ear, "how on earth do you know the way to Szentendre?"

Bertie glanced at her over his shoulder and grinned, the sun ricocheting off his white teeth and barley-blond hair. "I was an airmail pilot for a time," he explained, his voice just rising above the roar of the wind. "I've delivered post all over the continent."

"Good lord, how old are you?" Flora asked, peering at her companion through her goggles. It didn't seem entirely possible that a man without even the slightest hint of a wrinkle could have had such a plethora of experiences.

Bertie simply smiled at her and turned his eyes back to their invisible path.

The clouds cleared, and as she looked down Flora observed a world in miniature. Grassy fields; russet trees; and muddy tracks surrounded the neat farms nestled amongst the hills. Streams cut their way through the hibernating land and roads wound around it, giving passage to the occasional tractor but otherwise sitting in sleepy contentment. There were few towns and even fewer people, and Flora had the distinct feeling that she was in fact Odysseus, drifting on the crest of a wave between strange and foreign worlds. They were, Flora realised, following a wide grey river as it snaked through the countryside beneath them, passing over the towns and cities which sprung up along its banks. It could only have been the Danube, and she gazed down upon it greedily, eager to remember every detail.

Flora was not of a romantic disposition and rarely evinced marked enthusiasm of any kind, yet this river had featured particularly prominently in the mythologies of her early childhood and she was finding it almost impossible to maintain her usual standard of sophisticated detachment. Her father had learned to sail on this river; her parents had spent their honeymoon drifting upon it in Laszlo's yacht; and her mother had passed the first idyllic year of their marriage trying to capture its mysteries in oil-paint. Indeed if Beatrice was to be believed, Flora understood that she had even been christened on the banks of the river in Szentendre – although that all sounded a little too Old Testament to Flora's sceptical ear, and she had her suspicions that that particular anecdote was the product of the absinthe she and her mother had been drinking when the revelation had been shared.

"Not long now," Bertie cried, "keep your eyes peeled for a landing spot."

The aircraft drifted gracefully back down to earth, and Flora drew a cigarette from her bag and tucked it between her lips in preparation their imminent landing. As a mark of the increasing friendship she felt for Bertie, Flora even popped a spare in the corner of her mouth in case he should want one; an honour which, to date, she had only ever bestowed upon Alice. Flora peeked over the side of the plane and watched with interest as the town below grew in size. Houses swelled from their pin-head beginnings; the cobbled streets filled with small people; and the lush fields grew into handkerchiefs, then pillow-cases, then recognisable farmland surrounding the town.

"This will suit us very nicely," Bertie announced, as the aircraft dropped smoothly into a field to the south of the town and taxied under the cover of overhanging trees.

"Beautifully done," Flora commended as Bertie killed the engine and looked back at her with a broad smile on his face, ruddy from the effect of the wind. The pair sat there in companionable silence, enjoying their cigarettes and the stillness in the air now that the propeller was no longer whirring away in front of them.

"We should be about a mile outside of Szentendre by my calculations," Bertie said, jumping down into the long grass and helping Flora with her dismount, "which means that we'll be in time for an afternoon coffee and slice of Dobosh if we walk briskly."

"Now, Bertie," Flora said, removing her hat and goggles and drawing a comb through her flattened curls as her escort retrieved their bags, "it really was extremely good of you to bring me all this way, but I'm afraid that I shan't be able to offer you much in the way of hospitality. I hardly know what I shall find up at the castle - at best I suspect that it shall be eggs for supper and unaired sheets to sleep on. You're more than welcome to stay this evening, of course, but I shall have to get to work tomorrow."

"My dear girl," Bertie said, "say no more. I should like to see you safely to the castle, if you don't mind – I'm afraid my Pater promoted Arthurian standards of chivalry – but I'm certain that there will be an inn with accommodation in town. It has been an absolute joy to have a chance to take Cynthia-Rose for a spin, and that's quite enough for me."

"I must say," Flora replied, as the pair made their way out of the field and towards the nearest road, "that it is so....*comfortable* travelling with you. You seem to know just what to say."

Bertie laughed at that and offered Flora his arm. "Now then," he said, looking up at the sun to get his bearings, "let's find this castle of yours."

Bertie and Flora made their way up the winding road towards Szentendre as the sun began to set behind them. They were passed by a solitary farmer with a horse and cart who tipped his hat when Flora wished him a "good afternoon" in flawless Hungarian, but otherwise they were quite alone in their pleasantly bucolic scene, and looked for all the world like a young couple returning from a bracing wintry picnic. Bertie's calculations were perfectly accurate, and they soon found themselves walking across cobbled streets and past apricot-coloured houses. The baroque cross stood proudly in the middle of the main square, and people bustled about them as the scene began to slip from afternoon to evening. As they made their way into the town, Flora spotted a middle-aged woman in a red head-scarf sweeping the step outside a bakery, and wandered across to her.

"Excuse me, madam," Flora said, enjoying the feeling of the Hungarian words in her mouth and trying to erase the traces of her immaculate English accent, "I wonder if you could tell me the way to the Medveczkys' castle?"

The woman looked up at the exquisite girl standing before her, and narrowed her almond-shaped eyes as she tried to place her. "Do I know you?" she asked, leaning on the broom handle. She was a slim woman with a pretty face; an excellent advertisement for her bread, Flora thought.

"I haven't been here for many years, so I suspect not," Flora replied with a slight smile. "You may have known my father, Lazslo Medveczky, or my uncle Antal? I am Anasztázia Medveczky."

The woman's mouth fell open and she stared at Flora in astonishment. "Well I never," she said after a moment. "Victor!" she shouted, turning around and looking into the shop, "Victor, come out here!"

"You seem to have caused something of a stir," Bertie said into Flora's right ear, as the baker emerged out of his shop.

"What is it?" Victor said crossly, marching towards his wife.

"This is Lazslo Medveczky's daughter," the woman said, confident that her words would have the desired effect on her irritable spouse, "Anasztázia."

The baker pulled off his cap and scratched his balding crown, whistling between his teeth and looking down at Flora. "Is it now," he said eventually, obviously much taken by this revelation. "Well, I'll be."

"She's looking for the castle," the woman said, planting her hands on her hips.

The baker grunted, and continued to stare.

"You tell that uncle of yours that he owes us fifty pengö," the woman said to Flora now, wagging a small finger at her. "He's a devil when it comes to settling his tab."

"I'll be sure to do so," Flora said smoothly, wondering where on earth her uncle could have shuffled off this mortal coil if the locals hadn't got wind of it. "So, the castle...." she prompted, looking hopefully at the pair.

"You can't miss it," Victor said, replacing his cap and folding his burly, floury fore-arms. "Follow the road out of town, take the first path on your right and walk about half a mile."

"I don't know what sort of state you'll find it in, mind," Victor's lady wife warned them, pursing her lips and patting the bun which was beginning to escape from her head-scarf. "That uncle of yours hasn't been in town for weeks now, and from what I hear the housekeeper has turned to drink. *Again.*"

"In which case, we'd best make sure we have provisions before we set off," Flora said brightly, not in the least deterred by this announcement; in fact she was rather comforted to hear that the castle was unlikely to be dry. "I wonder if you might have a loaf of bread we could purchase? Dear Uncle Antal always says that you make the finest bread this side of Paris, and it would be such a treat to have some for our supper."

"Well," the baker's wife said, flushing with pleasure and bustling her husband inside with the broom, "it is true that my husband has a god-given talent. I'm sure we can find something – can't we, Victor?"

The baker had ceased his ogling in order to march back into his shop, intent on finding his astute young customer a prize loaf. He returned within seconds, clutching to his chest a golden brown disc in the manner of a proud father.

"I can see my uncle didn't exaggerate your talents," Flora said, extemporising wildly, "I can't remember when I've seen such tempting bread." She accepted the loaf from the elated baker, and smiled sweetly. "I'm afraid that I have no money with me, but I shall be back tomorrow if you wouldn't mind waiting?"

"Not in the least," the baker replied magnanimously, conveniently forgetting that Flora was the near relation of one of his least reliable customers.

The baker's wife looked to be a touch put out by the way in which this beautiful young stranger had so quickly captured her husband's heart, and she peered at Flora through narrowed eyes. "Now don't you forget to remind your uncle that he owes us money," she said rather tartly. "We're running a business here, not a charity."

"I shall be sure to pass that on," Flora said, taking Bertie by the arm and guiding him away from the pair. "Thank you so much for the bread, you're a darling." This parting comment was directed at a positively glowing Victor who gazed back at her in adoration, much to the irritation of his wife.

"I say, what was all that about?" Bertie asked as they followed the road away from the square and towards the far end of town. "That woman looked as though she'd swallowed a lemon."

"It would appear that my uncle has run up something of a debt," she explained, tucking the bread in her satchel and glancing up at Bertie with mischief in her eyes. "And I was also flirting quite shamelessly with her husband."

Bertie threw his head back in laughter. "I thought as much – he seemed a shade flustered." After giving himself a moment to enjoy his mirth, Bertie looked down at Flora, a curious expression in his blue eyes. "I can't speak Hungarian, so forgive me if I have got completely the wrong end of the stick here – but did you tell the baker and his wife that your name is Anastasia?"

Flora pulled a pair of cigarettes from her bag, and returned his look with her steady gaze. "Anasztázia," she said. "I was christened Anasztázia Flora Medveczky. My mother switched my names after my father died – I think she thought it would be easier for me at school if I didn't sound like the child of someone who'd fought on the wrong side during the war."

"It's a beautiful name," Bertie said as he lit their cigarettes and handed one to Flora. "It suits you."

Flora smiled. "Thank you – I'm certainly very fond of it, although I rarely use it these days."

They drew some very interested glances as they walked through the river-side town; Bertie because he looked so decidedly English, and Flora because with her wide-hemmed trousers, scarlet lips and cashmere scarf she oozed the kind of urbane sophistication many of the young women of Szentendre longed to achieve. The river slipped in and out of view as they walked up the gentle hillside, and Flora looked for it eagerly whenever they approached another clearing. After ten minutes or so, Bertie took Flora's arm as though in affectionate familiarity, and drew her slightly closer to him.

"Don't turn around," he said quietly into her ear, "but we've been tailed since leaving the bakery."

"Really?" Flora asked calmly. "By whom?"

"Two men in long black overcoats," Bertie replied. "One of them is rather short and appears to be wearing sunglasses - an odd choice for a November dusk, I must say – and the other is about six foot and has a long duelling scar on each cheek. Sound familiar?"

"The second sounds rather like one of the new joiners in upper fourth," she replied in her deadpan way, although her interest was piqued. "Perhaps they're just enjoying an evening stroll?"

"It's entirely possible," Bertie conceded, "although I think that I shall keep an eye on them."

They carried on walking away from town and turned up the small track, as instructed by the baker and his wife. Flora stole a glance over her shoulder as they rounded the corner, and saw that the two men were swiftly closing the gap between them. "They certainly appear to be headed in the same direction as us," Flora observed, trying to make out how far they were from the castle in the fading light. Bertie looked unusually stern, and his grip on her arm was tightening.

"Follow me," he said quietly, edging off the path and towards a small clump of trees not ten yards away. He fell to his haunches and pulled Flora down next to him. "Let's watch them for a moment," he whispered, his shadowy face only inches from Flora's.

Flora slowed her breathing and stared out into the rapidly fading light, her eyes straining to make out the shape of the two figures as they moved inexorably towards them; the Scylla and Charybdis of Szentendre, she thought to herself, rather pleased that she was still able to recall her Homer in such strange circumstances. The sound of hushed voices reached her before her eyes had a chance to adjust, and she felt Bertie's body stiffen as he listened on.

"They're German?" Flora asked, looking up at Bertie.

He nodded curtly. "German, and up to no good."

"Can you understand them?" Flora whispered, leaning even closer to Bertie to ensure that her voice didn't carry.

He nodded again, holding a finger to his lips as he tried to make out what they were saying. His mouth thinned, and the normally smiling eyes looked grim as the voices grew louder.

"The one with the scars is asking the shorter man whether they should kill the girl, or bring her in for questioning." He paused again as the foreign voices drifted through the still evening air. "And the shorter man is saying that it depends entirely on whether she decides to cooperate."

"Is he now," Flora said, an edge of steel in her hushed voice. "I presume they're talking about me."

Bertie's face retained its hard expression. "Wait here," he said suddenly, standing up and moving silently towards the road and the two Germans.

She looked on in astonishment, before drawing the pistol out of her bag and stalking noiselessly after him.

The two Germans continued up the path, assuming, no doubt, that Flora and Bertie were still making their way towards the castle. Their quiet chattering continued, and Flora wished that her German was as fluent as her Hungarian. As it was she could make out the odd word, but as they were mostly prepositions she hadn't the foggiest idea what any of it meant.

Without warning Bertie suddenly burst out of the bushes, seizing the shorter man and pinning his arms to his torso.

"Don't move," he growled in German to his captive's scarred companion, as the man made to draw something from the depths of his vast coat. "If you do, I'll kill your friend here." Up close the duelling scars were extremely disconcerting, giving the man's already razor-sharp cheekbones a welted prominence. The German's ice-blue eyes stared at Bertie with fierce intensity; unlike his diminutive friend he was built along extremely impressive lines. None of this seemed to disconcert Bertie, though, who was displaying remarkable sangfroid, it seemed to Flora.

The pinioned man turned purple with frustration and began shouting maniacally to his companion, his sunglasses now askew on the bridge of his nose. Flora's German may have been rudimentary, but even from her spot in the undergrowth she could hazard a guess that he was telling his friend to shoot Bertie, and therefore raised her own pistol in readiness. She was pleasantly surprised to find that she felt entirely relaxed. If anything, she was simply rather irritated that they were being harangued after such a long journey, when all she wanted was a gin and tonic and a long soak.

"Now then," Bertie said, rather loudly for Flora's benefit, "I assume that you speak English?"

The captured man continued to wriggle and shout, but it was clear from Flora's hidden vantage point that Bertie was holding him in a vice-like grip. She hadn't expected it of her new friend, but at that moment he really did look reassuringly dangerous.

The taller man with the scars narrowed his eyes, and nodded curtly at Bertie.

"Good," Bertie said, coldly. "Now would you mind telling me why you are following us? And why you have been discussing the possibility of killing my friend?"

The would-be murderer sneered. "Your friend?" he asked in a clipped German accent, raising his thin eyebrows for dramatic effect. "I think you are in arrears, sir. We were deciding whether or not we should have pork for supper, not whether or not to kill a woman. Schweine, fraulein – I can depreciate how the confusion can have arisen if German is not your native tongue."

Flora snorted at the German's extraordinary mangling of the English language, and wished for a moment that Alice could be there to enjoy it with her.

"My good man," Bertie replied in flawless German and with a wolfish grin, "I spent much of 1930 studying Nietzsche in Munich. Let me, then, assure you on two counts. First, my German is excellent. Secondly, I - unlike you it seems - have never confused a young lady with a farmyard animal. If you make a habit of that, sir, no wonder you are sporting such livid scars."

The German snarled, withdrew something from the depths of his jacket at lightning speed, and lunged at Bertie. A silver blade flashed in the moonlight; a deafening report cracked through the silent evening; and the German crumpled to the ground. Both Bertie and the smaller man (still locked in Bertie's arms) looked up in amazement as Flora emerged out of the undergrowth, pistol in hand. The alleged pig-fancier ground his teeth in pain as blood seeped through the fingers clasped tightly over his right shoulder.

"Flora?" Bertie said, rather taken aback.

"You should get him to a doctor," Flora commented, ignoring Bertie's surprised stare and looking to the wounded man's small companion. "I'm perfectly happy to shoot anybody about to lunge at a chum with a knife, but I'd rather not have your friend's death on my hands. The paperwork would doubtless be extremely tedious."

The smaller man adjusted his sun-glasses and wriggled free of Bertie's slackened hold. "Do as she says," Bertie said. "And tell your superiors what happens to scoundrels who skulk about in the shadows threatening schoolgirls."

"Former schoolgirls," Flora interjected. "As soon as I've taken my Cambridge entrance exam next month, I shall be a free agent."

"My apologies, Flora," Bertie said, his lips twitching as he offered her a small bow of apology. "Soon-to-be-ex-schoolgirls," he amended.

The two Germans listened to this exchange in bewilderment, and began to suspect that the English couple were not of entirely sound mind. "Lunatics," the short one muttered, before scraping his comrade off the path and doing his best to prop him up. Bertie stepped forwards, apparently struggling with the idea of letting the pair return to town when they had so obviously intended to cause Flora harm. Given that the only alternative seemed to be murdering them both in cold blood, however, he thought the better of escalating his intervention and restrained his baser instincts.

They made an odd pair as they shuffled down the road in the lengthening shadows, the taller man wincing with every step and the shorter staggering under the weight of his wounded friend - together forming a kind of two-headed, hunch-backed monster. Flora looked on dispassionately, gun at the ready in case one of the Germans should suddenly turn on them, and she and Bertie waited until they had disappeared from view entirely before returning to their hiding place to retrieve their hamper, and bags.

"You were rather handy back there," Flora observed, taking a well-earned swig from her hip-flask and offering it to Bertie. "Let me guess – you were a prize-fighter in a previous life."

Bertie grinned down at her, savouring the heat of the Oban whisky. "Basic military training," he replied vaguely. "I told you I'd been in the Navy."

"Hmmmm. I always thought sailors were more au fait with knots than wrestling," Flora mused, her face the picture of innocence. "However no doubt you would need to be fairly robust to manage the oars."

Bertie chuckled; he knew full well what Flora's father had done for a living, and was quite sure that she was being facetious.

"I must say, you weren't exactly slow off the mark yourself," he retorted. "Where did you learn to handle a gun?"

"Endless Glorious Twelfths trudging through muddy fields," she replied, swinging her bag over her shoulder and making her way back to the path. "And Alice has a water pistol."

"Well, I'm jolly glad you've had all that practice on the grouse," Bertie said ruefully, following her through the bushes. "I'm sure I'd look like a pin-cushion by now if it wasn't for your quick reactions."

"The knife!" Flora cried, looking about where her victim had fallen, "I saw him drop it, Bertie. I suppose we oughtn't to leave it lying about."

Bertie pulled a small torch from the hamper and cast its rays slowly across the dirt track. An owl hooted in a nearby tree, and Flora drew Pongo's scarf a little closer around her shoulders. Brave she may be, but even Flora wasn't entirely immune to the combination of shock and cold. "Oho, here it is," he said after a quick search, sinking to his haunches to retrieve it.

"What's that?" Flora asked, pointing with the hip-flask to a symbol embossed on the leather handle of the cruelly-serrated blade.

"That, Flora, is a swastika," he replied grimly, wrapping the knife in his handkerchief and placing it carefully in the hamper. "It's the insignia of a political party in Germany called the National Socialists. Adolf Hitler's mob."

"Yes, I've heard of them," Flora said gravely. "What in heaven's name could a pair of Nazis want with me?"

"I have absolutely no idea," Bertie replied, a frown wrinkling his smooth forehead. "But it may be that this castle of yours holds a clue." Whatever Flora may have thought of this development, she kept her own counsel and sipped her whisky in silence.

The duo carried on up the path guided by the light of Bertie's torch, like Dante and Virgil cautiously treading the road into the underworld (if Dante had been smoking a cigarette, and Virgil singing show-tunes in a surprisingly vibrant baritone). Barely five minutes had passed when a vast, gothic structure loomed out of the darkness before them, replete with turrets and, if Flora's eyes did not deceive her, a moat. Swirls of moonlit cloud curled around the castle's shadowy peaks, a cold fog rose from the grass, and the sounds of nocturnal hunters rustled in the undergrowth.

"Cosy," Bertie said cheerfully, not to be deterred by this Polidorian apparition.

"I'm sure it looks quite lovely in the sun," Flora retorted with only the slightest hint of hesitation.

As they made their way closer the building began to look decidedly less austere, much to their shared relief. The castle was hewn from a warm grey stone which glowed amber in the moonlight, and possessed two conical towers between which sat numerous peaked roofs of differing heights; a host of leaded windows betraying no sign of life; and what appeared to be an ornamental garden surrounding the moat. Eventually the dirt-track merged into a gravelled drive-way and they found themselves edging towards the end of their journey.

"Good lord, is that a *Buick*?" Bertie exclaimed, directing Flora's attention to a very smart burgundy car perched on the other side of the moat.

"I suppose it could be," Flora replied noncommittally, smoothing her hair and making sure that her gun was properly tucked away. Cars had never really been her line – she could never understand the male fascination with engines and horsepower.

"What an absolute beauty," Bertie said

They crossed the drawbridge (across what was, in fact, a very modest moat), their footsteps crackling across the gravel, and approached the vast, dark wooden door. Flora glanced up at Bertie, exhaled quickly and pulled on the thick coil of rope hanging in front of her. The sound of a distant bell echoed faintly in the belly of the castle, and the pair waited expectantly. The seconds passed, the ringing faded into silence, and nothing happened. Flora rubbed her hands briskly against the arms of her jacket, and shivered slightly as the cold night drew in around them.

"We need to get you inside," Bertie said, looking down and noticing that Flora was beginning to shiver. "There must be somebody there." Striding forwards with great determination, Bertie gave the rope three firm tugs. "I used to be a bell-ringer for my village church," he added. "If that doesn't rouse them, then nothing will."

Again they waited, and nobody stirred. "Well, I vote we head back to town," Bertie said. "There's no point in freezing to death out here. I think I spotted a promising looking little inn in the market square."

Flora looked distinctly unimpressed with his capitulation; after his display with the Germans, she would have expected rather more spirit. "I suppose that would be the sensible thing to do," she conceded. "However, there must be an open window here somewhere. The baker's wife definitely said something about a housekeeper, so the place can't have been totally abandoned. Particularly if there's a car parked outside. I'm sure she wouldn't mind if we let ourselves in...I am family, after all."

"Well....alright," Bertie said, after a moment. "We'll try the break-in. If there isn't an obvious way in, though, I say we go in search of hot food and beer."

"Agreed," said Flora.

The pair began to circle the castle, looking for any door or window which had been left ajar. Even with Bertie's torch it was difficult to make anything out in the darkness, and they were on the cusp of abandoning hope when Flora let out a small cry of triumph.

"I knew there'd be a way in," she declared, pointing to a first floor window above them and turning a beaming smile on Bertie.

"It's higher than it looks, Flor," Bertie warned, rubbing his chin in thought.

"Nonsense," Flora replied scornfully. "My upper fourth dorm room was higher than that, and Alice and I climbed in and out of that often enough."

"Well," Bertie conceded, "you might just reach it, if I pop you up on my shoulders."

"Fine," Flora said without hesitation, dropping her bag and limbering up. "Let's give it a go."

Bertie put his hands against the stone wall, and fell down to his haunches. "Stand on my shoulders," he said, "and I'll stand up very slowly."

Flora removed her shoes, and hopped across the cold earth in her stockinged feet. "Ready?" she asked, placing her right foot gingerly on Bertie's broad shoulder.

"Up you go," he replied cheerily, holding on to her ankle and waiting for her to put her second foot in position. Slowly and with great care, he raised himself to his full height with Flora balanced above him, her hands resting against the wall for balance. "That's as far as I can go," he said at last, pleasingly without the least hint of strain in his voice. "Can you reach?"

Flora stretched her hands outwards, and slipped them through the crack of the window three inches above her head. Easing it open as carefully as she could, she gripped on to the window frame and looked down at Bertie. "Let go of my ankles," she asked confidently. "I'm going in."

"Careful there," he said, letting go as instructed and leaving his hands hovering by her legs in case she should lose her footing.

Flora braced her arms, made sure of the placement of her hands and, finding a couple of uneven stones with her feet, pushed herself up until she was able to ease her torso towards the window. She slithered easily through the gap, dropped down onto the carpeted floor below and immediately tried to acclimatise her eyes to the darkness. She could hear a grandfather clock ticking somewhere nearby, and the kinds of creaking which were the hallmark of any old building - otherwise, the room was silent. She leant out of the window and waved at Bertie. "I'll let you in at the front door," she announced, disappearing immediately from view.

As soon as she was out of the room, Flora paused to orientate herself. She reasoned that she must be in one of the tributary corridors that fed into the first floor landing, and tried to steady her breathing as she made her way past the row of closed doors and towards the atrium at the heart of the castle. When she reached the landing she was able, in the half-light cast by the moon, to make out a solid wooden staircase and a thick carpet of indeterminate colour; the Catherine Morland in her had half-hoped for glinting suits of armour and perhaps even the odd mace or broad-sword, but that gothic vision was, alas, seemingly not to be. At least her ancestors were looking down upon her from a series of imposing portraits – that would have to do.

Flora walked across to the head of the stairs, placed her hand on the ornately carved bannister and made her way down to the front door. Arriving on a wide Turkish rug which covered the stone floor she froze mid-step, thinking that she could hear a muffled sound in the half-darkness, before persuading herself it was nothing and moving forwards to let Bertie in.

"And what do you think you're doing?" a husky, rather slurred voice demanded in Hungarian.

Flora screamed and spun around to find a plump woman of advanced years standing in front of her in shapeless, calf-length cotton dress, faded grey socks which had slipped down to her ankles, and a pair of fluffy slippers. She was holding a weak torch, clasping a woollen shawl around her shoulders, and eying Flora suspiciously through a pair of bleary, myopic eyes. The creature also emitted a distinct aroma of schnapps, causing Flora to recollect the caustic references made by the baker's wife to Uncle Antal's house-keeper.

"Flora!" Bertie bellowed, having heard his companion's blood-curdling cry and hammering insistently on the door. "Is everything alright in there?"

"Fine, thanks," Flora shouted back to him. "I think I've found the housekeeper!"

The elderly woman continued to scowl suspiciously, and advanced towards Flora holding her torch like a bludgeon. Flora smiled as sweetly as she could. "Hallo," she said in Hungarian with a slight laugh, holding her hands out to show that she was unarmed, "I'm Anasztázia. Laszlo Medveczky was my father."

The old woman sneezed, coughed and glowered at Flora. "Baron Medveczky died years ago," she replied, still staring at Flora with eyes full of mistrust.

"Yes he did," Flora agreed, speaking very slowly as she suspected that the woman was not entirely lucid. "Luckily for me, not before I was born. Uncle Antal sent for me."

Mention of her uncle seemed to go some way towards mollifying the woman. "Mr Antal asked you to come here?" she asked, tipping her head back and shining her torch into Flora's face in order to get a proper look at the girl.

"He did indeed," Flora said, raising a hand in a bid to make this exchange feel rather less like an interrogation. "As I say, I am his niece. And may I ask who you are?"

This seemed to take the woman back somewhat, and she lowered her torch. "I am Magda," she announced with pride. "I take care of the castle."

"Well, it's a huge relief to find you here, Magda," Flora said breezily. "Now if you don't mind, I shall open the door so that my guest can come in out of the night air." Before Magda could respond Flora had stepped forwards, turned the key, and removed the plank of wood sitting in brackets on either side of the door and barring Bertie's entrance. "We'll also require two beds to be made up, if you would be so good."

Magda's mouth gaped to reveal her largely toothless gums, and she stared at Flora in a mixture of awe and outrage. It was many years since she had actually been asked to *do* anything (Antal had spent a great deal of time abroad, and when he was home subsisted mainly on bread and cheese) and whilst she admired Flora's evident power of command, she certainly didn't enjoy the memories of servitude her tone aroused.

Bertie bounded through the open door, handed Flora her bags, and nodded at Magda in greeting. Flora fished a cigarette out of her case, placed it between her teeth, and was on the verge of striking a match when it occurred to her that perhaps she ought not expose this ethanol-soaked woman to a naked flame; the local doctor would no doubt have his hands full already with the winged German.

"This is Magda," Flora said in English, clasping the cigarette between her small, perfectly white teeth until such time as it became safe to smoke.

"Hallo there, Magda!" Bertie said brightly, offering a hand to the housekeeper in a very cheery display of bonhomie. The sight of this friendly, extremely handsome foreigner seemed to calm Magda's sense of doom - even though she could not understand a word he said - and she shook his hand with something approaching coquetry.

"I shall see about your beds," the housekeeper announced grandly to Flora, prepared now, having seen Bertie, to ensure that they had a comfortable night's sleep. "I shall also light a fire in the library."

"Thank you," Flora replied graciously. "I wonder if there's anything to eat?"

"Pickled cabbage," Magda said with a sniff, her flurry of goodwill fast exhausting itself. "And perhaps some potatoes. Although I make no promises."

"Never mind," Flora replied stoically, thanking whatever benevolent deity had given her the foresight to procure an emergency loaf of bread. "I don't suppose we have any gin?"

"No gin," Magda announced, as she prepared to hoist herself upstairs to try to identify in which nook she might have stowed the linen. "There's schnapps. And Mr Antal has some brandy in the library."

This was excellent news, indeed. As Magda made her way upwards, muttering darkly under her breath and coughing violently after ever five or six steps, Flora and Bertie began to explore the ground floor in search of the library. After trying several doors which appeared to lead into a variety of morning rooms; drawing rooms; store cupboards and closets, they at last found their sanctuary. Bertie managed to find a light-switch by the door, much to Flora's relief; she had feared that it might be nothing but candle-light for the foreseeable future - which was all well and good for a quiet supper à deux, but less helpful in the midst of a mysterious jaunt to the continent featuring murderous Germans.

"Magda said there ought to be some brandy in here somewhere," Flora said, scanning the room for a likely decanter. "Keep your eyes peeled."

"Aha!" Bertie cried in triumph, raising a bottle of Armagnac in the air. "What shall we drink to?"

"Let's drink to you, Bertie," Flora said magnanimously, as Bertie poured two healthy measures into a pair of rather dusty crystal glasses sitting on the drinks cabinet, "and your excellent navigational skills."

"And to your eagle-eyed shooting," Bertie replied, returning the compliment and handing a glass to Flora.

Flora took a large sip, and sighed in contentment. "Now, Magda said something about a fire," she said, "but I have grave doubts about letting her anywhere near a box of matches. So I think I shall have a go." She walked confidently towards the wicker basket stacked full of logs by the fireplace and fell to her knees, crystal glass in hand. "Why don't you divvy up the rest of that pie and some of that bread?" she suggested as she began selecting some choice bits of kindling. "We can have a picnic."

When Magda entered the room an hour later, sweating profusely and feeling distinctly light-headed after the ordeal that was stripping and remaking two beds, she found the pair sitting by the light of a blazing fire, chatting happily and making short work of the brandy.

"There are rooms ready for you," she rasped, looking at the Armagnac with longing. "I'll bid you good night, then."

"You're a saint, Magda, thank you," Flora replied with a smile, feeling decidedly mellow and really quite pleased to be back in Hungary, upon reflection. "Szép álmokat."

Magda harrumphed and slouched out of the room, exhausted after her sudden burst of activity, but secretly rather relieved to have a Medveczky back in the castle once again. It had been a full month since Mr Antal had come home for a change of clothes and some Hungarian noodles, and she was beginning to worry for him.

"I think that I shall try to get some sleep," Flora said, pushing out of the nest of cushions they had arranged by the fire and getting to her feet. "Shall we go in search of our rooms?"

"If it's all the same to you," Bertie replied, "I intend to find a comfortable sort of chair and keep watch. We may have frightened those Germans off for now, Flor, but I don't trust them to stay away."

"Oh, Bertie," Flora said, decidedly touched by this display of chivalry, "I'm sure there's no need for all that. Besides, you need a good night's sleep before you fly back to England. Although," she added, suddenly struck by what Bertie had said, "perhaps we ought to do a last sweep – make sure there aren't any open doors we missed earlier, that sort of thing?"

Bertie nodded. "Alright. Bring your brandy."

The pair did a slow tour of the ground-floor, padding about in their socks and taking the occasional sip of brandy. Even in the darkness it was clear enough from rattling door-knobs and window frames that everything was secure. It also become quite obvious how large the Medveczkys' castle really was, given that the investigation took the pair the best part of half an hour. At last, satisfied that they were safe and with their glasses drained, the pair parted ways at the top of the stairs. It was an oddly awkward moment – they'd become rather good friends during the course of the day, and didn't quite know whether to hug, salute, or simply walk away. In the end, they settled on a firm handshake.

Bertie waited until Flora was safely tucked up in bed and snoring gently before dragging a rocking chair from his own room and assuming guard outside hers. He wouldn't sleep that night, but it was a sacrifice he was more than willing to make for his new friend.

FIVE

Flora was woken by the sound of a man crying out in the night. Sitting bolt upright in bed with a racing heart, her eyes darted about the strange room. It was still bathed in darkness, the only light offered by the slithers of moonlight finding their way in through the gaps in the curtains.

Flora swung her long legs out of bed and padded across the carpeted floor to her satchel, which was lying on a desk by the window. Seizing her gun, she wrapped herself in an oversized silk dressing gown she had found hanging in the wardrobe, pulled a pair of what were presumably her uncle's thick socks over her bare feet, and slowly opened her bedroom door. Bertie's empty chair stood immediately in front of her and she very nearly crashed into it before freezing mid-step, looking up and down the corridor for signs of movement. Satisfied she was alone, she carefully edged past it and towards the landing.

It had sounded like the cry had come from the floor below and so, employing the considerable powers of stealth she had developed during numerous furtive cocktail parties at St. Penrith's, Flora crept down the wooden stairs and began her hunt.

The castle was silent once again, and Flora pressed herself into the shadows as she moved silently from room to room. She began her search in the library, somehow hoping that it was Bertie who had emitted the cry, after stubbing his toe on his way to help himself to another brandy. The room was empty, only just illuminated by the dying embers of the fire. Edging her way back out into the hall, Flora hovered in the moonlight and listened closely. As she stood motionless, her back pressed against the wall and pistol at the ready, her experienced ear suddenly detected the sound of a match been struck. Squinting against the darkness, she was just able to make out a small glowing flame burst into life through an open doorway on the other side of the staircase. With her pistol held raised in front of her and the belt of her dressing gown firmly knotted in place, Flora crept across the stone floor and prepared to confront whoever might be standing in the shadows beyond.

Her struggling eyes were just able to make out the shape of a person crouching down in the centre of the room, with their back to her and holding a lit match in their hand. Without hesitating she flicked on the light and raised the weapon, fervently hoping that she would find nothing more than a soused, somnambulant housekeeper.

"Good god!" she said, as an astonished Bertie leapt up and spun around to reveal a lit cigarette perched between his lips and a poker in his hand. At his feet lay the lifeless body of the shorter German assassin, a pool of black blood gathering around his head. "*Bertie!*"

Springing into action, Bertie placed the poker on the light blue carpet and moved towards Flora. "I hoped you wouldn't have to see this, Flor," he said grimly, as he guided her towards a chair and offered her his cigarette. "I'm afraid that we've had an uninvited guest."

"What happened?" Flora asked, finding it almost impossible to tear her eyes from the dead man's inert body. "Are you alright?" She wasn't a squeamish girl, but this was the first time she had seen the aftermath of a violent death, and Flora found that she was extremely grateful to be sitting down.

"Yes, I'm fine," he replied, scanning the room. "Although I wouldn't have been if this little devil had had his way." Bertie looked down at the revolver curled in the dead man's hands, and shook his head in disgust.

Noticing her discomfort and the way the colour had drained from her face, Bertie tried to position himself in front of the German's head, and very quickly suggested that they should adjourn to the library.

"I'd love to, Bertie," Flora replied as calmly as she was able, "however I fear that I am not entirely in command of my legs. They seem to have turned to jelly."

Without saying a word Bertie took the gun from her hand, gathered her up, carried her across the hall and deposited her very gently in an arm-chair by the dying fire in the library. It was all done in the most business-like manner, and rather than feeling herself overcome by the kind of giddiness which would surely have affected many eighteen year old girls clasped in Bertie's strong arms, Flora found that she was instead jolly grateful for his quick thinking and practicality. "Thank you," she said, smiling at him as he poured a brandy from the decanter and handed her the glass.

"Not at all," Bertie replied, helping himself to a glass and pulling a second cigarette from his pocket, which he lit with an admirably steady hand. "If you feel up to it, my dear, I ought to explain what's been going on."

"Please do," Flora replied, having recovered sufficiently to find herself suddenly gripped by curiosity. "I must say, though Bertie, that if *this* is what it's like to spend an evening with you, please remind me never to accept an invitation to one of your parties."

"That's the ticket," Bertie said with a slight grin, appreciating Flora's very swift return to form. Pausing to puff on his cigarette and collect his thoughts, Bertie eased himself into a chair opposite Flora and began to talk.

"It was like this, Flor. After you'd gone to bed I dragged a chair across the landing and positioned myself outside your door. It was tolerably comfortable - I think I even nodded off once or twice, I'm afraid - but shortly after the clock in the hallway struck two, I heard a noise; creaking hinges, that sort of thing.

In any case, it sounded as though it was coming from the hallway, so I crept over to the staircase to investigate. Once I reached the landing, I could see a faint light moving around below me. I half thought that it might be Magda, but it seemed impossible that she could be making so little noise. So, I came halfway down the staircase and pressed myself into the shadows, watching as the light drifted from room to room. It appeared very much as though the person was looking for something, since he didn't spend very long in each room and was moving at considerable speed. Eventually the light moved into your uncle's study, and didn't come out again for some time. I slipped the rest of the way down the stairs, and snuck in after him. And that's when I realised that it was one of our German friends come to visit."

Bertie paused to refill Flora's glass, then to reach for a blanket which was lying on the sofa behind him. As the shock of seeing the body wore off, Flora was beginning to feel the biting cold which gripped the castle at night, and her teeth were chattering like castanets: the blue silk dressing-gown, whilst undoubtedly beautiful, didn't offer much protection from the elements. Bertie draped the blanket around her shoulders and peered down at her. "Are you alright, Flora?" he asked anxiously, rubbing her upper arms. "We can always finish this tomorrow," he reassured her. "Perhaps we ought to get you back to bed; I can take care of the body."

"This dressing gown is rather thin, that's all," Flora said matter-of-factly. "And I certainly won't be able to sleep until I know what happened. Do go on."

"Alright," he said through narrowed eyes. "But you must promise me you'll go to bed if you feel you need to."

"I promise," Flora promised, her eyes gleaming with amusement. This paternal side to Bertie was really very endearing.

"Now where had I got to?" he asked, as he returned to his own seat. "Ah yes - discovering the German. As I was saying, once I'd followed the intruder in to the study I was able to recognise him very quickly as our friend from earlier this evening. He was leaning over your uncle's desk and rifling through his papers; Lord knows what he was looking for, Flor, but I can tell you that he seemed extremely agitated.

Well, after our previous encounter I thought that I had better arm myself – so as he was facing the window and had his back to me, I crept over to the fireplace and picked up the poker. We carried on in this way for some minutes — the German frantically turning out your uncle's drawers and me standing there with my weapon, feeling like a bit of a lemon – when I decided I ought to intervene; bring the thing to a head, you know. So I cleared my throat and asked the German what he bally well thought he was doing. Obviously I gave the poor fellow quite a shock, because he jumped half way to the ceiling and swore with considerable violence as soon he saw me standing there in the moonlight. I rushed forwards to restrain him, certain that he would have a gun about him somewhere, but I was too slow - he was already drawing out a revolver by the time I reached him. So I'm afraid I knocked him rather hard on the head before he had a chance to pull the trigger."

"I think that's when I must have heard him cry out," Flora explained.

"Almost certainly," Bertie replied. "He did let out quite a yell when he saw the poker descending towards him. I'm surprised Magda hasn't turned up as well, actually."

"Schnapps," Flora said briefly.

Bertie seemed to be both highly embarrassed at having killed someone during his first night under Flora's roof, and also rather proud of himself; it was not every day that one prevented both an assassination and a burglary, after all. For her part, Flora felt that this whole episode raised a number of troubling questions: what had the German been looking for; why did he and his partner want to kill her; and how the devil had he got in to the castle in the first place?

"Was there any sign of a break-in, Bertie?" she asked, drawing the blanket more tightly around her shoulders as she curled up into the chair and tucked her hands under her feet. "I distinctly remember checking that the front door was locked before we went to bed, and unless we missed something earlier I can't recall there having been another way into the building." She paused and pushed a stray curl behind her right ear. "I must say that I cannot like the idea of having murderous Germans waltzing in and out whenever they feel like it; it doesn't make for a particularly restful evening."

"I didn't notice anything," Bertie replied, "but then I was so focussed on keeping an eye on the intruder that I didn't really have time to work out where he might have come from. I rather think that we can deal with that in the morning," he concluded, very sensibly. "Unless there is an inexhaustible supply of Nazis in Szentendre, I would be very surprised if we were to encounter any more disturbances this evening."

"I'm sure you're right," Flora concurred, by now feeling ready for her bed. "What shall we do with the body, though? It would give poor Magda a real shock to stumble across it in the morning - and we already got off to a slightly rocky start, what with me breaking in."

"Leave that to me," Bertie said, getting to his feet and making for the door. "I'll be back in a jiffy."

Flora heard the key in the front door scrape against the lock, and felt a gust of cold air blow into the library as Bertie made his preparations. She burrowed more deeply into her chair, closed her eyes, and waited. He couldn't have been gone for more than fifteen minutes, yet Flora fell into a heavy sleep in his absence. Alice, who had watched Flora sleep through numerous raucous fire alarms and even once during the school orchestra's memorably strident (yet woefully inaccurate) performance of The Ride of the Valkyries, would not have been surprised.

His task complete, Bertie locked the front door once more and returned to the library. "Flora," he whispered, shaking her very gently, "the thing's done." As this didn't rouse her, and, not wanting to give her a fright by resorting to more energetic tactics, Bertie gathered Flora in his arms for the second time that evening and carried her up the stairs. Once he had tucked her safely into bed, Bertie resumed his watch outside her room and waited for dawn.

SIX

Flora awoke the following morning sprawled across the magnificent four-poster bed, feeling remarkably refreshed. For a moment the events of the previous night were forgotten and she was able to enjoy the sensation of waking up in a new place, far from the tedium of school life. She looked about her in amusement at what could only have been a man's room: there were no ornaments; no cushions or clusters of potions on a dressing table; almost no clothes in the wardrobe and only one token picture of a stag on the wall. As she stretched her limbs and spotted the thick woollen socks on her feet, the image of the dead German leapt back into her consciousness. Flora grimaced, then thought for a moment. It was absolutely essential that she should discover how the man had got into the castle, why it had been so important to him and what on earth he had been hunting for; like all individuals who've spent their formative years in a British boarding school she was fiercely protective of her own space, and didn't take kindly to foreign men snooping about her family home whilst she slept.

Flora hastily dressed herself and pulled a comb through her hair before making her way downstairs. Trills of laughter filled her ears as she reached the hallway, and to her astonishment she was greeted by the image of Bertie and Magda standing side by side in the study, both wreathed with smiles. Magda, who the previous evening had resembled a kind of pickled Medusa, had clearly made an effort for her male guest: the wild grey curls had been replaced by a neat bun; the baggy socks and shapeless clothes had been exchanged for a smart blouse, ankle length skirt and clean apron; and where the scent of schnapps had reigned the previous evening, a powerful floral perfume now held sway.

"Morning, Flora!" Bertie cried, "I was just trying to explain to Magda here that I dropped a bottle of red wine all over the carpet last night, hence the stain."

Flora looked down at the carpet to find that the corpse had indeed been replaced by an empty bottle of Burgundy, which seemed to have leaked over what had once been a puddle of blood. The smell of fine wine permeated the air, and it would have been very easy to believe that her sighting of the dead German had been nothing but a horrible nightmare. With a small shrug of the shoulders and a rueful smile, Flora explained in her perfect Hungarian that Bertie had had a small accident the previous evening.

"It doesn't matter," Magda replied, smiling up at Bertie in a distinctly flirtatious manner, "Mr Antal is very understanding about these things."

"It really seems," Flora said to Bertie, switching back to English, "as though nobody knows about my uncle's death but me. Lord only knows where it happened. I don't know whether I ought to say something."

"Perhaps not, for the time being," Bertie replied thoughtfully. "It would only upset the poor woman – and besides, until someone actually finds his body and reports it, there's always the hope that it was a false alarm."

"I have prepared breakfast," Magda proclaimed, ushering Flora and Bertie towards the door. "Come – I will show you to the dining room."

"I must say, I'm jolly glad you're here," Flora said to Bertie out of the side of her mouth, as they walked behind Magda like a pair of naughty children. "There's no chance she'd be this accommodating if she hadn't completely lost her head over you."

"Well, she's only human, after all," Bertie replied with a broad grin.

Magda led them into a spacious dining room situated at the back of the castle, overlooking the hills beyond. The vast mahogany table in the centre of the room could easily seat thirty people, and the stone fireplace - in which, Flora was relieved to see, Magda had lit a large fire - was wide enough to house two deer-hounds standing nose to tail quite comfortably. The stone floor was covered in richly coloured rugs, and the morning sun, which was already shining through the tall windows, succeeded in making what could have been rather an austere room look pleasant and welcoming. On the long table standing at the opposite side of the room to the fire-place, Magda had set out a smorgasbord of cold meats, cream cheeses, pâte, breads and scrambled eggs.

"Magda!" Flora exclaimed. "This is absolutely wonderful! Did you go down to town this morning to get all of this?"

Magda shrugged and muttered something under her breath about Hungarian hospitality and what Mr Antal would expect.

"Lord, you're an absolute treasure, Magda," Bertie said, advancing on the food with the light of intent in his eyes, "would you tell her, Flora?"

"Bertie says you are a veritable jewel," Flora said to the housekeeper, who promptly flushed red to the roots of her hair and left the room.

The pair piled their plates high, and made themselves comfortable at the end of the table closest to the fire.

"I tell you what," Bertie declared, tucking in to his meal with gusto, "if this is what it's like in Hungary then I will seriously have to consider finding employment in this neck of the woods."

"I can see that," Flora replied with a quick smile. "And I'm sure Magda would be delighted if you could stay a little longer. Are you planning on flying home this morning?"

"Home?" Bertie cried in disgust, "Good lord, Flora, you can't think that I would leave now? Abandon you here with Germans skulking around the place? What sort of flat tyre do you take me for? And besides that, there is obviously a first rate adventure to be had!"

"Certainly not a flat tyre, Bertie," Flora retorted. "You've been an absolute rock, but this is obviously a dangerous enterprise which has nothing to do with you. There's no reason for you to risk your life on my account. Besides, I don't think Beatrice would forgive me if anything were to happen to her new model."

"Well, I like that," Bertie said indignantly, letting his knife and fork clatter to his plate, "and here I was thinking we were friends."

"Well of *course* we're friends," Flora replied, "but what I'm trying to say is that you needn't feel as though you were obliged to stay. I'm perfectly capable of looking after myself, you know."

"I don't doubt that for a second," Bertie countered. "However I should very much like to remain for my own sake, as much as anything. I haven't had so much fun in ages. Of course if you'd rather I leave..."

"Oh, don't be so silly, Bertie," Flora said, dismissing this out of hand. "I'd be delighted if you stayed, but I don't want you to feel as though you're obliged to, that's all. And I certainly don't want you to get hurt." This final admission rather slipped out, but Bertie took it with his usual air of unfailing cheerfulness and simply smiled broadly at her.

"That's settled then," he declared rising and returning to the side table to reload his plate. "Where do you think we should start?"

"By finding out how that snoop got in," Flora said decisively. "Unless we can find a broken window or some kind of side door that has been forced, it would appear to be a mystery. Before we get to that, though," she added, wandering across the room to help herself to coffee, "what did you do with that body?"

Bertie blithely continued to pile food onto his plate, and said simply that it was all "taken care of."

"Yes, but how?" Flora insisted. "Will Magda stumble across the body next time she goes outside to hang up the washing? Is there now a shallow grave in the middle of the ornamental garden?"

"No, no, nothing like that," Bertie reassured her. "He won't be found, I promise you. Not unless you're a particularly keen snorkeler, at any rate." This final caveat was said rather more quietly than the rest of the sentence, but Flora seized upon it at once.

"My god, Bertie, you flung him in the moat!"

Bertie chose neither to admit nor deny this charge, and simply buttered another slice of bread with an innocent expression on his face.

"I hope you weighed him down," Flora commented, practical as always. "The last thing we need is a bloated man floating about by the drawbridge."

This drew a reluctant chuckle from Bertie. "Of course I weighed him down," he reassured her. "I shan't go into the details at the breakfast table, but do bear in mind that I was in the Navy, Flora."

"I suppose I should be grateful you weren't in the airforce," she responded irrepressibly, "or we may have found him lashed to one of the turrets."

As soon as they had finished their breakfast the pair did a tour of the ground floor of the castle, searching for broken windows and hidden side doors. Despite spending a very thorough couple of hours checking every inch of the place, neither Bertie nor Flora were able to unearth so much as a draught: there were other doors into the castle of course, but they were all securely locked and bolted. They did, however, find a series of unusual objects which spoke to the idiosyncratic hobbies of the late Uncle Antal, including a lobster pot, a pair of stilts, a parachute, an engraving kit, a sniper rifle and a collection of wigs. "If it wasn't for those Germans, I'd suspect that my uncle was having me on," Flora said, rather gingerly holding a false moustache aloft by the tip. "He seems to have been something of an eccentric."

Bertie slipped a navy blue fedora on his head and, doing his best Clark Gable impression, suggested that they should talk to Magda.

They found her in the kitchen, quietly peeling potatoes and singing a folksong to herself. Seeing the pair coming down the stairs towards her, Magda hurriedly tried to remove the bottle of schnapps from the centre of the wooden table; Bertie was too quick for her, however, and managed to demonstrate through a kind of semaphore that he would like to try some. A surprised and slightly hesitant Magda poured a small measure into two tumblers and handed them to her visitors. Bertie went first, tipping the clear, fiery liquid into his mouth and swallowing it in one. His blue eyes swam with tears but he managed not to cough, and even raised a smile: this, in Magda's eyes, was the pinnacle of virility. Flora, who rather prided herself on being able to hold her drink, gasped with shock as the home-made spirit trickled down her throat, wheezing as she placed the glass back on the table.

"Good lord," she said, eyeing the bottle with renewed respect. "Magda, that stuff's vicious. I shall have to procure a bottle for Teddy."

The housekeeper grinned with pleasure, inviting the young pair to sit down now that they'd passed the test. "Can I help you?" she asked.

"I hope so," Flora said, taking a seat opposite Magda. "Do you happen to know," she began slowly, wondering how best to phrase her question without giving too much away, "whether it might be possible for someone to gain entrance to the castle if all the doors and windows are locked?"

"Of course," Magda said with a nonchalant shrug of the shoulders, as though it was the most obvious thing in the world.

Bertie drew up a chair next to Flora and watched this exchange with interest, wishing that he could speak this utterly impenetrable language.

"Really?" Flora asked in surprise. "Could you show us?"

With a small sigh, Magda relinquished her knife and pushed herself away from the table. "Come on then," she said, shuffling around the table and back up the stairs.

Flora was rather taken aback by the speed of these developments but quickly hurried after Magda, keen to pursue any lead.

"Does she know something?" Bertie asked, as they made their way back up to the hallway.

"It would seem so," Flora replied. "D'you know, I haven't been this riveted since Miss Waverley's production of Medea: The Musical."

In no time at all Magda had led them to the coat cupboard next to the library. Flinging open the doors, Magda pushed the coats aside and stepped inside, stamping on the floor until she could hear a hollow echo. "Aha," she cried, before bending down and pulling up what appeared to be a trap-door, "there you are."

Bertie pulled his torch out of his pocket, and quickly shone the light into the small cavity. "Stone the crows!"

he cried, replacing Magda in the back of the wardrobe, "It's a secret passage, Flora!"

Bertie put the torch in his mouth and started climbing down the small metal rungs leading down into the darkness. "This is marvellous!" he cried in delight through his clenched teeth, as his head disappeared.

"What is this, Magda?" Flora asked the housekeeper, half-wondering what other surprises this strange old castle might have in store for her.

"Just an old passage," Magda replied with another nonchalant shrug. "Your father and uncle used to play in it all the time when they were boys."

"And where does it lead?"

"The top of the path leading to town," Magda answered, smiling suddenly as Bertie shouted up muffled words from the dark hole below. "There's another trap-door there, but it's mostly overgrown now. I don't think anybody has been down there for twenty years."

"And do people in town know about it?" Flora wondered, stepping into the cupboard and looking down into the tunnel. "I must say, this is all rather Lewis Carroll," she muttered in English.

"Oh yes," Magda replied, "everyone knows about the tunnel. I'm sure half the men in the village have been down in it – your father used to charge an entrance fee." She chuckled fondly at the memory, shaking her head as she began to make her way back down to the kitchen. "Such a clever little boy."

When Bertie didn't reappear Flora assumed he must have decided to see how far the tunnel could lead him, so she settled herself in the library with a glass of wine and a novel. Just as she was managing to lose herself in Barsetshire (it turned out that the castle was very well stocked with a selection of both English and Hungarian classics), he came crashing through the front door, rather damp and covered in ivy.

"I say!" he declared, bounding into the room, his cheeks flushed and his blonde hair in disarray. "What a thing to have in your house – it leads all the way to the road, Flor!"

"So I hear," she replied cordially. "Did you enjoy it?"

"I should think I did," he agreed enthusiastically, sitting down opposite Flora and lighting a cigarette. "It's absolutely foul down there – particularly when you go under the moat. Very slimy."

"What was the trap-door like at the other end?" she asked, abandoning Trollope and accepting a cigarette from Bertie. "Was it terribly over-grown?"

"Not a bit of it," Bertie said. "There were plenty of loose leaves, but it looked as though someone had trimmed it all back very recently."

"Then I think we have discovered the German's way-in," she said through narrowed eyes. "In which case, I'm inclined to put something very heavy on that door as soon as possible."

"I thought you might say that. I spotted a likely looking stone statue of one of your rellies in the hallway – I'll just drag it across."

"Thank you, Bertie," Flora replied, bestowing a dazzling smile of gratitude upon her friend. "And then let's go and have a poke around in the study; I've patiently waited for your return before heading in there, which I hope you will agree was extremely generous of me."

Half an hour later (and once Bertie had discovered that life-sized stone statues were, in fact, a touch heavier than he'd anticipated) the pair ventured into the study, intending to find out why Flora had been instructed to return to Hungary, and what their uninvited visitor had been looking for. In light of the German's nocturnal preoccupation with the desk that seemed like the sensible place to start, and Bertie and Flora spent a very industrious two hours reading through every scrap of paper stuffed in its drawers or strewn across its red leather top. Apart from an abandoned novel written in the Proustian style (the opening line – "He awoke, not remembering if he'd wept some tears for his lost youth, or no tears at all" filled Flora with embarrassed horror, and she'd swiftly tucked it back into its drawer); a sheaf of bills from Victor's bakery; a collection of very amorous letters from a woman called Anaïs; and an invoice from a picture framing shop in Budapest, the desk yielded little of interest.

"What could he have been looking for?" an exasperated Flora asked, letting another graphic declaration of love from Anaïs flutter to the floor and wishing, not for the first time, that she had had the foresight to bring tea-bags. "Other than the fact that my uncle appeared to subsist solely on loaves of bread and was, by all accounts, a neglectful lover, I've discovered absolutely nothing. Perhaps he simply asked me to come to help establish some kind of filing system."

"It would indeed appear as though this is a dead end," Bertie conceded, sitting back on his haunches and lighting a cigarette. "At least we know that the German was looking for something which would typically live in a desk, Flor. What could it be?" he wondered. "A letter? A key?"

"Perhaps the Germans weren't political spies at all," Flora mused. "Perhaps, Bertie, they were extremely efficient bureaucrats who had heard of the anarchy existing in this study and decided to take matters into their own hands."

Bertie smiled at that, and eased himself into a chair with a sigh. "Did your uncle say anything else in the telegram which could be of help to us? He can't have expected you to get to the bottom of this mystery without some kind of clue, Flora."

"All he said was that I needed to come to Hungary as soon as possible, and that it was obviously curtains for him if I received his message." She paused to light a cigarette, and collapsed into a chair. "Oh, and he asked me to thank Beatrice for the portrait of my father, and said it needed reframing."

"What?" Bertie cried, leaping to his feet, "Well that's it, Flor! It must have something to do with that picture!"

"You think so?" Flora asked, suddenly excited. "It doesn't look particularly mysterious, Bertie. Father does look very handsome, though – I'll say this for Beatrice, she may be a touch unreliable as a mother, but she's a very fine artist."

Bertie followed the direction of Beatrice's eyes, and looked up at the portrait on the wall.

"So that's your father," he said, looking up admiringly. Beatrice's picture showed a square-jawed hero looking down at the daughter he had never known: clear blue eyes smiled lovingly at the artist; the olive skin was burnished by the sun and touched by the beginnings of laughter-lines; and fine brown hair was swept across a strong brow. He was wearing his naval uniform, hat perched at a jaunty angle on his head in the manner which, unbeknownst to Flora, had landed her maverick father into trouble with his superiors on numerous occasions. Four hundred years earlier it would have been the face of a dashing pirate; as it was, Beatrice had captured the vibrant spirit of the husband she had known for such a short period of time, and loved beyond measure.

"It is indeed," Flora said simply, knocking the ash from her cigarette and looking up at the painting. "I can't see what the Germans would want with him, though."

"My guess is that your uncle has hidden something tucked behind the canvas," Bertie said, walking across the room and gazing up at the portrait. "Would you mind if I take a look?"

"Of course not," Flora replied, quickly joining him next to the fire-place.

Bertie clambered up onto a chair and reached for the painting.

"I say, this is all rather reminiscent of Richard Hannay, Bertie," Flora observed with a laugh, as Bertie stretched up onto his toes and reached for the picture which they hoped would solve the Szentendre mystery. "I wonder if there's some kind of a code painted into father's eyebrows."

Bertie lifted the portrait from the wall and stepped carefully off the chair back onto the carpet. "Right," he declared, pulling a pen-knife from his pocket and turning the picture face down, "let's take a look at it, shall we?"

"Do be careful, Bertie," Flora cautioned, feeling suddenly rather protective over this testament to her parents' affection for one another.

"Never fear, Flor," Bertie replied. "I worked in my mother's gallery for a summer after I left school, so I'm quite used to handling canvases."

"Of course you did," Flora said placidly, accepting this addition to Bertie's growing armoury of skills with equanimity. "Can I do anything to help?"

"Shine my torch on the knife," he instructed her. "That's it."

Very delicately and displaying great patience, Bertie removed the picture from its wooden frame. He managed to execute the task without causing any harm either to the frame or the painting, and Flora breathed a sigh of relief as Bertie propped the canvas against the arm-chair.

"Lord, Uncle Antal was quite right," she said, looking down at the heavy frame in disgust. "It really is the most appalling frame – poor Pa."

"I don't understand it," Bertie said in consternation, pressing his fingers against the back of the canvas and fixedly inspecting the frame. "There's nothing here."

He sounded so wretched that Flora was moved to place a comforting hand on his shoulder. "Perhaps Uncle Antal tucked something inside the frame itself?" she suggested, peering down at the teak monstrosity. "Is it hollow?"

Bertie picked the frame up and tapped his knife against the wood, generating a dull thudding sound. "It's absolutely solid," he said dejectedly. "What a bore."

They sat there next to the fire-place, looking down at the disembowelled portrait and wondering whether they had let their imaginations run away with them. The most likely explanation was that whatever the German had been looking for was tucked away in another drawer somewhere in the castle; hidden behind moth-eaten socks and abandoned linens. Why, Flora thought to herself, would her uncle go to all the trouble of constructing some kind of elaborate parlour game if he had needed her help as urgently as his telegram had suggested? She was on the cusp of getting to her feet to make her way back into the library and find Anthony Trollope, when her eye was caught by the strange blood-burgundy stain in the corner of the carpet.

"Alright," Flora continued, persuaded by the evidence of a recent death to suspend reality a little longer, "Let's think about this clue another way. Perhaps Uncle Antal wasn't talking about the image itself – perhaps the painting of my father is just a sign-post." She looked across at the opposite side of the room, and at the picture which had faced her father. "Let's take a look at this one."

Abandoning Laszlo, the pair rushed across the room and seized the nondescript sketch of a frozen lake hanging opposite the space where Beatrice's painting had been. Bertie plucked it out of its metal frame and eagerly ran his fingers across the canvas. Finding nothing he turned to the frame.

"This one's hollow," he said, glancing up at Flora. She nodded at him, and he prised the four sides of the frame apart, shaking each one in turn and shining his torch into the dark cavities.

"Well?" she asked, leaning over his shoulder and trying to get a glimpse into the metal tube.

"Nothing, I'm afraid," Bertie said, dropping the piece of frame and switching off his torch. "We're missing something, Flor – something elemental. I'm convinced that the answer is staring us in the face."

Flora took Bertie by the hand and dragged him to his feet. "I vote that we sleep on it, and resume the hunt tomorrow," she said. "I often find that answers to knotty problems present themselves to me after a good night's sleep, and I don't think that we will achieve anything by carving up Uncle Antal's art collection."

"Of course you're right," Bertie replied with a rueful smile, slipping the knife back into his pocket and pulling a rogue piece of ivy from his sweater. "It's intensely irritating not to have solved the thing, though."

"Yes it is, Bertie," Flora agreed, patting his arm, "however just think of all the progress we've made today. You, for instance, have disposed of a body; found a passage under a moat; and hit upon the crucial clue in my uncle's telegram. And I," she continued, looking up at her friend, "have made it through the first three chapters of *The Warden*, which I have been trying valiantly to do for the past year."

"Are you enjoying it?" Bertie asked conversationally, as he reassembled the portrait of her father.

"Very much," she replied. "I always think that Victorian novels are going to be such a trial – it must be something to do with those heavily bearded, rather grim author photographs – but I am almost always wrong and this is proving to be no exception. The legal profession and the press are both being absolutely skewered."

"My father wanted me to be a lawyer," Bertie remarked, as he reinstated Laszlo in his position on the wall. "I told him that I couldn't imagine anything more soul-destroying than being bound to a desk all day reviewing the dense verbiage of over-paid administrators. And then I ran away to Kenya."

"I feel sure Trollope would have approved," Flora assured him. "Shall we go through to the library and have a cocktail before supper?" She was extremely glad to see her mother's picture restored to its place once more, and felt that that alone deserved a toast. "I wonder if Magda has got any ginger ale - I'd kill for a horse's neck."

It transpired that Magda did indeed have a stock of ginger fizz in the pantry, since Antal was also partial to that particular drink. "I think that we'd have been great friends," Flora said with a small sigh. "Everything I learn about my uncle makes me like him more. Although I must say that he treated poor Anaïs *cruelly*."

Magda deposited the bottles on the drinks trolley in the library and was preparing to return to the goulash she had been working on all afternoon, when Flora asked her to stay a moment longer.

"I wonder, Magda, could you describe Uncle Antal to me?" she asked, as Bertie handed her a drink and lit her cigarette.

The housekeeper paused for a moment. "He was very tall," she announced. Apparently she thought that this would sate Flora's curiosity, and she made to leave the room once more.

"Hold on, Magda," Flora called out with a laugh, "couldn't you tell us a little more than that?"

As Magda edged back into the room and racked her brains for the kinds of details Flora might want, Flora translated this exchange for Bertie.

"Now," Flora said, "what was…is he like? You know, his personality?"

The question rather perplexed Magda. She had worked for the Medveczkys for more than forty years, yet she had never had cause to assess the characters of the members of the family before; they were just….who they were, she thought to herself impatiently. She wrinkled her nose and twisted her mouth, desperately trying to call to mind anything which may distinguish her employer from any other forty year old Hungarian aristocrat.

"Well," she began, "he is very like Laszlo to look at – perhaps half an inch taller, and with slightly darker hair. He has a scar on his chin," she said, smiling fondly, "from fighting with your father when they were both very small. Very bookish, like Laszlo – they always had their noses in books, those two."

Magda paused for a moment, to allow Flora to put this into English for Bertie.

"He has always been a very good master," she continued, warming to her theme, "he never raises his voice and always makes sure I have my afternoon off. On *Wednesday*s." Magda was sure to stress this last point for Flora's benefit. "Mind you, he's been away a lot lately," she added, looking slightly troubled. "There have been lots of hushed telephone conversations in that study of his, and last minute trips to I don't know where. He says it's to do with that book he's been writing," - Magda's voice was thick with scepticism; evidently she did not think a great deal of Antal's literary aspirations – "but that always sounds like balderdash to me. Besides,

I'm sure Mór Jókai's housekeeper didn't have to provide clean socks for foreign jaunts at a moment's notice."

"Has he told you anything about an important piece of paper?" Flora asked hopefully, wondering whether her uncle would have entrusted Magda with whatever it was he was hiding. "Perhaps a letter…a map…something like that?"

"Paper?" Magda repeated with evident surprise. "No, nothing's been said about any paper – other than that I'm not to throw away any of the pages of that blasted book of his whenever I'm allowed in to clean the study – which is not very often, let me tell you."

For a fleeting moment Flora wondered whether the Proustian novel held the key – perhaps her uncle had filled it with coded references for her, rather like Wilfred Owen's postcards from the front? Had she been on to something with her gag about *The 39 Steps*? This all struck her as being remarkably far-fetched, not to mention a great deal of work for her uncle (who must already have been fighting a daily battle to keep on top of Anaïs's endless correspondence), however she decided that it must be worth another look.

"Thank you, Magda," Flora said. "That's very helpful."

"I don't suppose he's told you when he's coming back?" Magda asked as she made her way to the door. "It would be nice to have some warning, and he'll only complain if he has to sleep between unaired sheets."

Flora felt a quick pang of guilt. "No, I'm afraid he hasn't told me," she replied, despising herself for the deception. "What time's supper?"

"It'll be ready when it's ready," came the gnomic reply from the departing housekeeper.

As soon as Magda had left, Flora retrieved her uncle's manuscript from the study. "She said that this is the one thing my uncle asked her not to touch," she explained, flicking through the type-written pages once more, "so I wondered whether he might have employed some kind of…code, you know."

The idea, once articulated, sounded ridiculous to Flora, but Bertie didn't laugh.

"It must be worth a read," he replied, forever the optimist. "I'm afraid that I won't be much help though, Flor – not with the thing being in Hungarian."

"He does use the odd English word, though," Flora observed. "And actually, there's absolutely no reason for him to have known that I speak Hungarian – I was barely a year old when we left."

"In which case, why is your Hungarian so good? I've been meaning to ask."

"Beatrice, god bless her," Flora replied with a smile. "Her Hungarian is hopeless, but apparently she thought that if I could speak the same language as my father, we'd have a connection of sorts. So she found a Hungarian émigré in Cambridge, and has paid for me to have lessons with him every week for the past ten years. It's the one thing I've really worked at," she explained, her eyes fixed on the manuscript. "It's such a beautiful language, you see, and she was quite right – it is nice to have something tangible in common with Laszlo."

Flora seized a pad and pencil from the coffee table, and told Bertie to read out every English word he came across. "Let's see if there's anything in it," she said, finished her horse's neck and settling back into the armchair.

After taking a short break to enjoy Magda's wholesome goulash (which Bertie described as being one of the finest meals he had ever eaten, to Magda's intense delight) the pair eventually assembled a list of some thirty words.

"I warn you, Bertie, this does not look terribly promising," Flora said, her lips quivering slightly.

"Read them out, then!" Bertie cried, refilling their glasses with burgundy.

"Alright, but don't say I didn't warn you." Flora held the list up to the light of the nearest lamp and trying to keep her voice steady. "Rhododendrons; marzipan; shuttle-cock; tremulous; wicket; madrigal; rancid; bamboozle; Shylock and fudge. Should I continue?"

"Oh lord," Bertie gasped, his shoulders shaking with laughter. "How wonderfully obtuse!"

SEVEN

To their credit, Flora and Bertie did spend the rest of the evening trying to work out whether Antal's peculiar assortment of English words could be attempting to lead them somewhere. However as they suspected would be the case, it was either an impenetrable code or had absolutely nothing to do with Flora's visit.

"I'm completely done in, Bertie," Flora declared after two hours of putting every cryptic crossword methodology to the test. "I vote that we should go to bed, and come at this with fresh eyes tomorrow morning."

"Lord, what a relief to hear you say so," Bertie said, knocking back the last of his whisky. "I've gone cross-eyed, and never want to have to think about marzipan again."

The pair said their farewells on the landing, Bertie having decided that he could sleep in his own room now that the secret passage had been blocked. Flora settled into bed, and tried valiantly to make it through another chapter of Anthony Trollope before accepting defeat and falling back into her soft pillows.

She awoke some time later to find the castle silent and the room in darkness. After tossing and turning for half an hour she finally realised she wasn't going to go back to sleep for the time being. Clambering out of bed she stood there dressed in one of her uncle's shirts and his thick socks, feeling irritatingly alert. Try as she might, she couldn't shake the feeling that they had left the front door open, and that the wounded German was making his way across the bridge to the moat at that very moment. Logic told her that Magda had been locking that door every day for the past four decades and that was no reason that she would have forgotten to do so on this of all nights. As is so often the way, however, Flora's fears were amplified by the lateness of the hour and she couldn't calm her over-active brain. Sighing in frustration, she seized the torch which Bertie had lent her, retrieved the gun which she had returned to her satchel, and padded across to the door.

Flora had never been a person who enjoyed total silence, and the quietness of the castle unsettled her. It was therefore with some trepidation that she poked her head out of her room and checked the corridor for signs of movement. The castle was bathed in the grey light of the moon which cast long shadows across the carpet, but nothing stirred. The ticking of the grandfather clock in the hallway was the only sound, like the steady beating of the building's heart. Edging forwards, Flora held both the torch and the gun in front of her and made her way towards the top of the staircase, fervently wishing that she was fast asleep and dreaming. Without either the comfort of a fire or the nest of blankets on her bed, she shivered as she moved along the corridor; the ancient castle seeming to have the same ability as every boarding house she had ever lived in to harvest the cold.

As she was creeping past Bertie's bedroom, Flora froze. She could hear the faint murmur of someone talking, and not from downstairs – it was coming from behind his closed door. As quietly as she could, she pressed her ear against the door and tried to make out who was speaking, and what was being said; the castle doors were all thick oaken affairs, however, and whoever was talking was doing so sotte voce. The most she could determine was that the speaker was male. "*Was he talking in his sleep?*" she wondered, as the voice continued. With her heart in her mouth she turned the handle and pushed the door open a crack - thank God Antal had kept the hinges well oiled, she thought to herself, as the door slid soundlessly ajar.

"Nothing further to report, sir," she heard Bertie say. "I haven't been able to find the list yet – I'm beginning to doubt that it's even here."

Silence.

"No, sir, she doesn't appear to know what she's looking for." Another pause. "Not in my opinion, sir – she poses no threat whatsoever....Understood, sir. Out."

Flora felt distinctly sick, and for a moment didn't know quite what she should do. Evidently Bertie was a lying scoundrel; what was not clear, however, was who he was working for. "Doesn't know what she's looking for," she thought bitterly, "no threat whatsoever." Remembering that she had the revolver in her hand, Flora decided that there was no time like the present to confront the snake in the grass. Pushing the door open still further, she turned the torch off and edged into the room with the gun raised.

Bertie was crouched by the window, his unreasonably chiselled jaw and tousled hair illuminated by the light of the moon. He had drawn the curtain back and appeared to be tinkering with something in his picnic hamper. "Timeo Danaos," she observed in disgust, prompting Bertie to spin around and stare at her in alarm.

"Don't move. Bertie – if that is even your real name," she said coldly, the gun trained on his heart. "You've seen me use this before, so you know I'm quite serious."

"Flora!" he said, hands raised in the air, "this isn't...."

"I don't give a damn," Flora replied, trying to keep her voice steady. "It's perfectly obvious that you've lied to me. You pretended to be a friend. And yet here you are, skulking around in my family home with some kind of bloody wireless."

"Put the gun down, Flora, and I'll explain everything."

"I don't think that you're in a position to be issuing commands, Bertie," Flora observed, slowly cocking the gun. "Sit down over there." She gestured to a rocking chair next to the window, suitably far away from any of his bags or the rest of the furniture.

Bertie edged across to the chair, hands still raised. His usually animated demeanour had been replaced by something harder.

"Flora..." he tried again.

"Who do you work for?" she asked curtly, keeping the gun aimed at his chest. "A rival German faction? A private enterprise?"

"Good God, no," Bertie replied in disgust, lowering his hands in surprise. "I work for the British Government, Flor- we're on the same side."

"Your superiors seem to doubt that," she said dryly. "Poses no threat whatsoever? The perils of having a Hungarian father, I suppose."

"Of course I don't doubt you," he said, grimacing slightly when he realised what she must have overheard. "It's just protocol, Flora - Europe is on the brink of another war, and the fact is that last time round your father was on the other side."

"My father was a Hungarian naval officer," she said coldly. "Rather a different proposition to the Third Reich, I'm sure you'd agree."

Bertie sighed. "Of course it is, Flor - but you can't blame them for asking the question."

"Who precisely is it that I'm not blaming?" she inquired. "Or can't you tell me?"

"Not really," Bertie confessed, looking across at her. "An agency in London."

"How comforting," she said, moving across the room without taking her eyes off her captive to pinch one of the cigarettes sitting on his bed-side table. "And are you at liberty to tell me why you have been at such pains to insinuate yourself into my homecoming? Or is that confidential too?"

93

"Might I have one?" he asked, looking at the cigarette in her hand.

"Not until you've explained yourself," she replied curtly, using his lighter and pushing the rest of the packet into her shirt pocket.

He sighed. "I think you ought to know what we're dealing with here, Flora – I had hoped to keep you out of it as far as was possible, but those two Germans rather dropped you in at the deep end. Besides, your uncle obviously wanted you to be involved – for which he would have had his reasons."

Flora said nothing to this, but perched on the edge of the bed opposite Bertie, her face half hidden in darkness and the gun still raised in readiness.

"Your uncle was a very brave man, Flora. For the past three years he has been collating a list of…moles, if you like, Nazi sympathisers embedded in some of the most influential posts in Europe. Politicians; socialites; bankers; journalists; even some royals – they've all pledged their support to Hitler whilst continuing to live their normal lives amongst their countrymen. At present this does little more than demonstrate a shocking lack of judgment in some of our leading lights. If we go to war with Germany, however, which seems increasingly inevitable, this network of supporters could prove to be absolutely vital to Hitler's chances of success."

Bertie crossed his legs, and looked across at Flora who slowly began to lower her weapon. "Your uncle has essentially been posing as a Nazi sympathiser for the past three years, in a bid to collate this information. He told my superiors that this was his intention in the summer of '34, but in a bid to keep his cover as secure as possible said that he didn't want to communicate with us until his list was complete. We finally received word from him seven days ago."

"Shortly before I got his telegram," Flora said.

"Yes. We think that his position must have been compromised at the last minute, although we don't know how yet. Nor do we know why he involved you – although I suspect it's because you were the only person he thought he could trust."

Flora sat there in silence for a moment, trying to absorb the enormity of what this young man was telling her. "So," she said at last, very slowly, letting the gun hang by her side and getting to her feet. "I suppose everyone's now after this list of his – you, the Germans, and whoever else might have got wind of it."

"Precisely," Bertie said. "We weren't sure that the Germans were on to us until you and I bumped into that pair on the road, which obviously confirmed it. And the fact that they discovered your location so quickly rather suggests that there may be a double-agent in my agency, feeding all this information back to Berlin - which is partly why my boss was a bit jittery about your background."

Flora said nothing for a moment. "I think you had better come back to my room," she announced at last in a colourless voice.

"Good lord, why?" Bertie asked, rather stumped by this unexpected reaction.

"Because I should like a drink, and my hip-flask is in my bag."

And so the pair made their way silently down the corridor, neither speaking as Flora walked slightly behind her erstwhile friend, once again clasping the gun in one hand and the torch in the other. She closed the door behind him, inviting him to take a seat in the corner as she fished around for her whisky.

"I suppose your name isn't really Bertie," she said lightly as she poured him a drink. She was more hurt than she was letting on, but had decided to believe him. The idea that he would be lying about this too was almost too much to contemplate, and her instinct told her he was on her side. Devious, but on her side.

"No," he confessed, in some embarrassment, "it isn't."

"Am I allowed to know what it is?" she asked, handing him the glass and raising the flask to her lips.

"Not really," he replied, "but I think I owe you that at least. It's Frederick – my friends call me Freddie."

"Not too much of a departure, then," she observed smoothly. "I think that I shall continue calling you Bertie, if you don't mind – false identities are a step too far for me. Out of interest, is anything you told me true?"

"Yes, it was," Bertie said quickly. "I'm not Bertie Cavendish, but everything else I told you was true enough. The Navy; the vineyard; Nairobi; my father wanting me to be a lawyer...."

"The Cynthia-Rose?"

He grinned at her, relieved to sense the beginnings of acceptance in her voice. "Even the Cynthia-Rose," he promised. "Scout's honour."

"And my mother?" she asked, her eyebrows raised in inquiry.

"Well, I did meet her in the food hall at Harrods," he explained, shifting a little uncomfortably in his seat, "but it wasn't exactly an accident. We have had someone keeping an eye on the school for the past few days, you see, and I was informed once you were on your way."

"Good lord!" Flora cried in disgust. "Someone watching the school! Don't tell me Miss Baxter is in your pay – although it would explain her uncanny ability to know precisely where I am at all times."

Bertie laughed in spite of himself. "I've never heard of a Miss Baxter," he assured her. "Unless she's above my clearance level, I don't think that she's working for His Majesty's Government."

"Who then?" she asked, really rather keen to find out the identity of this supposed snitch.

"Do you remember that nice young man who gave you a lift to London....?"

"No," Flora breathed incredulously. "I don't believe it."

Bertie simply shrugged his shoulders and drank from his glass.

"If this is the sort of treatment you give to schoolgirls, then I jolly well hope that I never fall foul of this agency of yours," she said loftily, although she was secretly rather impressed. "It's positively chilling."

Bertie made no rejoinder, and Flora meditated over her whisky. "Poor Uncle Antal," she said at last. "What a thing to do."

"It was heroic, Flora," Bertie said gravely. "You should be immensely proud of him."

"And I am," she replied simply. "However unless we recover this list of his, his sacrifice will have been for nothing. I vote that we should tear this place apart tomorrow morning until we find the blasted thing."

"Ah," Bertie said, "about that..."

"Lord, what is it now?" Flora demanded. "Do you have orders to shoot me at dawn?"

Ignoring this sally, Bertie got up from his chair and walked across to Flora, holding his glass out for a refill. "I've been given orders, Flor," he said, looking at her in concern. "Apparently the agency has a new lead in Austria – it seems that your uncle had a close friend there, who may know something about the work he was doing. And if so, Antal may have told him some of the names from the list."

"That's rather unlikely, isn't it?" Flora asked. "If he wouldn't even report back to you, then why would have had shared that kind of knowledge with a friend?"

"We don't know that he did," Bertie replied, returning to his chair. "However in the circumstances, the agency feels that every possible lead is worth investigating." Bertie looked down at his companion. "I should like you to come with me, Flora," he announced rather suddenly. "I can't really bear the idea of leaving you here when that other German may still be knocking about in town – you'd be much safer with me, in the Cynthia-Rose."

This last statement was made rather gruffly, and it dawned on Flora that Bertie was not just being gallant, but perhaps even a shade affectionate.

"Oh, Bertie," she said with a short laugh, "that's very good of you, but I can't leave just yet. Uncle Antal wanted me to be here, so there must be something to find. Besides, if that German is still plotting an incursion then I need to be here to look after Magda. I'm sure that she's fully capable of looking after herself, of course – it may even be more sensible for me to fear for the German – but I can't bolt yet. See what you can find out in Austria, and I'll hold the fort here."

"I don't like it, Flor," Bertie said, clearly troubled by this turn of events. "I don't think I could forgive myself if...."

"If nothing," she said briskly, keen to nip this potentially sentimental conversation in the bud; it was not an exchange she wanted to have in her bedroom in the middle of the night - particularly when she was wearing grey walking socks. "I shall be perfectly alright. Now we will both need a good night's sleep before tomorrow, so off you go."

Bertie rose, and made for the door. "I really am terribly sorry, Flor," he said, with that crooked smile. "And I very much hope that when this is all over…"

"Good night, Bertie," she said, before shutting him out in the corridor.

EIGHT

It took Magda some time to come to terms with the idea that Bertie had to leave. When Flora had told her that he needed to get going she'd flounced out of the room and spent the next hour crashing about in the kitchen, causing as much of a disturbance as she could with a metal ladle and a saucepan. She also made sure to avoid him for the remainder of his stay: Magda hated goodbyes – she'd never let Antal or Laszlo see her tears when they'd disappeared off to school, war, or for married life, and she was damned if she'd start now.

Bertie and Flora, on the other hand, spent a final few hours turning the castle upside down in search of Antal's list. They flicked through books; upturned vases; looked under rugs - Bertie even began to clamber up into the chimney in Flora's bedroom, before realising rather sheepishly that Antal was unlikely to have been foolish enough to hide his piece of paper above his fire-place. Eventually they accepted defeat for a second time, and Bertie went upstairs to collect his things.

"I have made him a picnic," Magda declared grandly, emerging from her underworld to thrust a bulging food-parcel and bottle of excellent looking claret at Flora. "And you tell him to come back soon."

Without another word she spun on her heel and returned to her kingdom below stairs, determined to console herself with schnapps and a good rant to the oven about nothing in particular.

"Magda says goodbye," Flora said solemnly, handing the weighty package to Bertie once he reappeared with this things, "and asked me to tell you that you mustn't stay away long."

Bertie tucked the picnic into his hamper and looked down at Flora. "I've left the radio in my room," he told her. "If anything should happen just switch it on and it will connect you automatically to London."

"Bertie," Flora said, moved by this gesture in spite of herself, "what if you should need it? I'm sure that I shall be in no more danger here than you shall be flying into Austria. Besides," she added, unable to stop herself from a slight dig, "what would your commanding officer say if he knew that you'd left equipment with a potential German collaborator?"

"You *must* stop saying that, Flor," Bertie replied with a grimace. "It really was the most innocuous background check – imagine the grilling I got when they discovered I could speak fluent German."

"I'm only teasing you," Flora said, softening, and pushing him lightly on the arm. "Give my love to Cynthia-Rose. And do be careful, Bertie. Don't trust anyone – that's what Uncle Antal said, after all."

"Flora," Bertie began, suddenly serious as he and Flora walked out of the front door, "it's of the upmost importance to me that you don't think I fabricated our friendship. Notwithstanding the rather sobering circumstances, I've thoroughly enjoyed spending the past few days in your company. In fact," he added, taking a step towards her, "I should very much like to kiss you."

"And perhaps I might let you," Flora replied serenely, whilst taking a step backwards, "once this is all over. I don't think that it would do either of us any good, Bertie, to complicate matters when we need to focus our minds on toppling the Germans. If I've learnt anything from living in a girls' boarding house, it is that affairs of the heart are the most crippling distraction. Pongo, for instance, very nearly flunked her Highers because her young man was spotted holding hands with the barmaid from the Dog and Whistle. And I don't intend to make the same mistake."

Bertie threw his head back and laughed. "Well said, Flora," he said at last. "Let's shake hands, then, and I shall be on my way."

Smiling sweetly, Flora extended her arm and took Bertie's hand in hers. "Good bye, Bertie dear," she said lightly, before turning on her heel and walking back into the house. Like many of her comrades at St. Penrith's – and, indeed, the incomparable Magda - Flora despised goodbyes; the briefer the better, as far as she was concerned. Bertie was also the product of a rigorous public school education, and understood this implicitly. And so off he loped to the Cynthia-Rose, determinedly expelling thoughts of her cherry-red lips from his mind.

Magda's very audible protest against Bertie's departure had subsided and Flora stood alone in the silent hall, listening to the ticking of the grandfather clock and wondering what precisely she should do next.

"Right," she said aloud, walking upstairs to fetch her gun, "onwards." Fashioning a kind of holster from a pair of stockings, Flora slung the revolver down by her waist and resumed her search of the castle. She began, where Bertie had left off, in her bedroom. She had unearthed a record player at the back of the wardrobe earlier that morning, and spent a very pleasant hour flicking through her uncle's library and listening to jazz. The mysterious list was still nowhere to be seen, however, and so Flora made her way methodically from room to room, carrying the record player with her and bobbing gently as she scoured the place for clues, the revolver slapping against her thigh as she moved in time to the music.

She was quite right not to have kissed Bertie, she decided – the fact that she'd discovered that he was in fact a British agent was quite enough to be going on with. Flora had regularly spurned the advances of any young man at St. Penrith's for Boys courageous or cocksure enough to ask her to the pictures, or to a dance; one of her long-suffering admirers had even been so moved as to compose a sonnet praising her rare beauty before creeping across to the Girls' School to recite it under her dormitory window in the middle of the night. Flora had felt the faint stirrings of sympathy as Miss Pevensey had dragged him back across the moonlit lawn accompanied by a chorus of heckling from the younger girls leaning out of their windows - but really, she had thought, that wasn't at all her thing and she'd much rather they focused their attentions on Annette or Muriel, or any of the other girls longing for a sweetheart. Bertie, though, had intrigued her. It was not often that one discovered a naked spy in one's apartment, only to be offered a ride in an aeroplane and a jolly few days in the most extraordinary circumstances. No: far better, she thought, to keep him at something of a distance until the question of the list had resolved itself. Then, perhaps, she'd let him have another try.

Having searched in every hiding place she could think of, Flora was unable to shake the image of her father's portrait from her mind. If her uncle had guarded this secret of his so meticulously for the past two years, why, then, would he have made gratuitous comments about her mother's picture in the only message he ever sent her? It seemed nonsensical and, from what she had learned of him, starkly out of character. Flora lit a cigarette and stretched out on the dust-sheet covering the four-poster bed, tapping her fingers against her stomach as she tried to think. She brought the image of the portrait to mind, and concentrated on every detail: the dark wood surrounded her father's face, the copper piping sitting on the inside edge of the frame and catching the firelight; the confident brush-strokes of her mother's hand. Suddenly she sat up, her eyes widening in realisation.

"My god," she said aloud. "Of *course*." Dashing downstairs, Flora made her way into the study and peered at the frame, her face only inches from the wood.

The copper edging on the frame was decorated with a kind of intricate, swirling pattern - or at least that's what she'd thought when they had first examined the picture. As she stared at the wood the swirls gradually took on the shape of a cursive script. Flora gasped - and then the world went dark.

"Flora! Crikey, she's out cold, Teddy.... *Flora*! Can you hear me?"

"*There's a woman tied up and gagged in here!*" Teddy cried from the library. "What the devil is going on? Hallo? Do you speak English, madam? *I don't think she speaks English, Ali!*"

"She's opening her eyes!" Alice cried out in relief. "Flor? Can you see me, Flor?"

"Alice?" Flora asked in some confusion, feeling an incredible pain shooting down her neck as she moved. "Lord, my head hurts." She winced and sat up, feeling distinctly nauseous as she did so.

"Careful, there," Alice said, gently supporting Flora as she tried to stand, "don't rush yourself."

"What," Flora asked, gingerly turning to look at her dearest friend, "are you doing here, Alice?"

"I say," Teddy declared, charging into the room, "there's an extremely irritated Hungarian woman in the next room – as soon as I removed her gag she started screaming at me. I don't think she's best pleased. Ah, Flora!"

"Teddy?" Flora cried, recoiling as the sound of her voice rang in her ears.

"Hallo, old girl," he replied cheerfully.

Flora felt distinctly faint. Raising her hand to the back of her head she carefully probed the egg shaped bump, grimacing as she did so. And then realisation pierced the fog of pain. "Oh lord," she said quietly, staring at the empty space on the wall where the picture had been. Dashing out in to the hall as fast as she could, she ran out of the front door and looked frantically for signs of life. The Buick, she noticed grimly, was gone. In its place, however, was a very smart Beauford.

"Magda!" she shouted, running back into the house and almost bumping into the raging housekeeper who had by now emerged from the library. "Are you alright?"

"No, I am not," Magda declared, her face purple with rage. "That intruder tied me up! Not before I hit his damn sling as hard as I could, though," she added with blood-thirsty delight.

"What man?" Flora asked urgently. "Was he German? Tall? A duelling scar on each cheek?"

"Yes," Magda confirmed, her eyes gleaming with loathing. "That's the Ördög." She spat onto the stone floor in disgust. "You know him?"

"I shot him two days ago," Flora replied grimly, before swearing in particularly colourful Hungarian.

Magda looked at her with a new respect; first for the shooting, and secondly for the swearing.

"Did you see where he went?" Flora demanded, seizing Magda by the shoulders. "It's very important, Magda."

"No," the housekeeper replied, feeling rather wobbly now that the shock was beginning to wear off. "I heard him take Mr Antal's car, though – that foolish boy will insist on keeping the keys in the ignition."

"What the blue blazes is going on here, Flor?" Teddy asked, interrupting this flood of Hungarian. "Who would want to knock you over the head?"

"A German spy," she replied coldly.

"What?" Teddy and Alice cried in unison.

"Teddy, is that your Beauford?" Flora asked, looking up at him in urgent appeal.

"Indeed it is," he replied proudly. "About this spy, though, Flor...."

"Right," Flora said, groping for the stocking holster and finding with some relief that her revolver was still in its rightful place. "We need to *follow that German.*"

To her relief, Teddy and Alice readily grasped the urgency of the situation and charged out to the car without asking any more questions.

"Magda," Flora said, turning to the housekeeper. "You'll find a radio in a hamper in Bertie's room – turn it on and tell the person at the other end that the Germans have the list. Tell them that Uncle Antal had the names etched into the copper piping on the frame. I doubt they'll understand you at first, but just keep talking until they find someone who can speak Hungarian."

To her credit, and bemused as she no doubt must have been, Magda nodded in understanding and told Flora to be careful. "That German was a nasty piece of work," she said darkly. "If I see him again, I will shoot him."

"Not if I get there first," Flora replied. "Lock the door after us."

And with that she leapt into the back of the Beauford, and was off.

"Drink this." Alice poured a measure of brandy into a flask half-full of coffee, and thrust it into Flora's hand. It certainly helped to steady her, and to numb the throbbing pain at the back of her head.

"I have no idea where he might have gone," Flora declared, accepting a cigarette from her friend and desperately looking about her for signs of the Buick.

"There's only one road leading away from this castle of yours," Teddy reassured her. "Whoever this fellow is, he'll be heading west."

"Towards Germany," Flora said bitterly. "It's absolutely imperative that we catch up with him before he reaches the border." Realising that she was yet to establish how it was that her friends had turned up in her uncle's study, Flora turned to Alice.

"Now, Ali," she said, "would you mind explaining what you and Teddy were doing in my uncle's castle?"

"Oh, it's quite simple, really," her chum replied brightly. "Miss Baxter gave me the most shocking grilling the morning after your escape, demanding that I tell her where you'd gone, and with whom. It was such a bore, Flor, I can't tell you – she told me I was *gated* of all things, as though I were some naughty fourth former who'd skipped Games – so I called Teddy and asked if he'd come and fetch me. Well, as we were on our way to Oxford I had the most appalling feeling – as though you were in some kind of trouble. I really can't explain it, Flor - and you know that I'm not usually the superstitious sort - but it felt jolly real. When Teddy saw what a state I was in, he suggested that we should pop across in the Beauford to find you. And if it turned out that you were perfectly alright, we could make a holiday of it. He's such a darling." She laughed and ruffled his hair.

"I drove to Switzerland with my brother a couple of summers ago," Teddy explained, glancing back at Flora, "and Hungary was only a smidgen further. Besides, I've been in a spot of bother myself, and thought a continental jaunt would be just the thing."

"Spot of bother?" Flora asked, accepting a second brandy from Alice. "What have you been up to, Teddy?"

"He was caught distilling gin in his bathroom at College," Alice said proudly. "He calls it Fortesque's Revenge – it's really very good."

"I've got some in the back actually," Teddy said with a modest smile. "Thought you might like to try some, Flor. It makes rather a good martini, if I do say so myself."

"That was incredibly thoughtful of you, Teddy," Flora replied, extremely moved. "Thank you."

"Now, Flora," Alice said seriously, "never mind Teddy's gin, what on earth have you been up to? We had the devil's own time of it trying to find you – Teddy's got a smattering of French and my Italian's not too shabby, but it's been such a struggle – no-one speaks a word of English. We really could have spent *days* ambling aimlessly around Xanadu" - ("Szentendre," Teddy interjected cheerfully) - "as people just kept staring slack-jawed when I tried to get directions to the castle. Thank heavens I made you tell me your father's name during that game of truth or dare when we were in upper fourth, otherwise we'd really have been in the soup." She paused to light a cigarette. "My heart nearly stopped when we found you on the floor like that, Flor," Alice said, raising a hand to her chest and turning rather pale. "Just *too* awful."

Alice and Flora had always complimented one another rather well when it came to their emotional rhythms; whilst Flora had a tendency to lean towards a kind of implacable stoicism, Alice was something of a dramatist. Their friendship meant that they generally kept one another somewhere in the middle of this spectrum, and only rarely strayed into the extremities. Alice was sorely tempted to do so now, given the circumstances.

"It's rather a long story, I'm afraid," Flora confessed.

"Plenty of grub in the back there if you're hungry," Teddy announced before Flora had a chance to begin. "We picked up some *wonderful* saucisson when we were passing through France, and there's an excellent baker in that town of yours. I think there's some claret swimming around in under my seat, too, if you fancy a tipple."

"I hardly think Flora wants claret at a time like this," Alice retorted, remonstrating gently with her beloved bon viveur. "If anything, we ought to open the Riesling, what with all this talk of Germans."

Alice had said this in jest, but Teddy thought it was an excellent notion and invited her to climb into the boot to fetch it.

"Not until I hear Flora's story," Alice replied firmly. "Flor?"

And so Flora regaled her friends with her version of recent events, keeping half an eye on the road ahead at all times in the hope that she might catch a glimpse of the Buick. I won't regale you with a verbatim description of Flora's report, since to do so would repeat much of the past seven chapters and, I fear, test your patience. Instead I shall offer you a selection of Alice's reactions, from which you may adduce the highs and lows of Flora's narrative arch.

"Nothing but a bunch of grapes?....He flew you here?....In the arm? Well done, you!....I can't believe he was a spy, although it is rather romantic, Flor....My god, that's ingenious – although it sounds highly time-consuming…"

"So where is this Bertie fellow?" Teddy asked, rather liking the sound of this enigmatic adventurer.

"He should be in Austria by now," she replied, before lighting a cigarette and leaning as far as she could out of roofless car, scanning the landscape. "I can't see anything," she called back to her companions. "The thought that we might've gone the wrong way makes me feel quite ill."

"I really don't think we have, Flor," Teddy offered in reassurance. "If this fellow is heading back to Germany then he must be going this way. Stands to reason. And if he's not…well, we can only give the thing our best shot."

Fields sped past them, mottled with cows. Alice did eventually scramble into the back and locate the wine, but when even Teddy refused a glass, staring instead at the road with a particular intensity, it became clear that all three of them were suddenly feeling the weight of history upon their shoulders. It was up to them, then, an aspiring opening batsman for England (Teddy); a revolutionary with her eyes fixed firmly on Westminster (Alice); and a winsome enigma whose ambitions remained a mystery even to herself (Flora), to protect Britain. Not even the idea of a sandwich made from Victor's unparalleled bread could tempt them from their silent introspection, and Flora, who had so far managed to retain a remarkable sense of calm, began to feel rather under the cosh.

"Good lord, Flora, look!" Teddy cried suddenly, letting go of the wheel and pointing urgently towards a path veering off to the left not five hundred yards ahead of them. "Is that the car?"

Flora followed the direction of his finger and positively yelped with delight as she spotted her uncle's Buick. "Oh well done, Ted!" she cried, clapping him enthusiastically on the shoulder. "And is that smoke coming from under the bonnet?"

"It looks as though the German has over-heated it," Flora declared, applying the surprisingly advanced grasp of mechanics she had acquired from a former boyfriend in the Royal Air Force. "He's blown the ruddy gasket."

"Can you see him?" Flora asked as they neared the now useless vehicle. "Is there any sign of the picture?"

Teddy pulled the car to the side of the road and the trio clambered down, rushing over to the Buick. As they had each feared would be the case the car was empty, the only sign that the German had been there afforded by a nasty looking truncheon abandoned on the passenger seat – no doubt the weapon used to bash Flora over the head. Leaping up onto the driver's seat, Teddy scanned the horizon with the eyes of a practised huntsman; not for nothing was he reckoned to be the best detector of partridge in Sussex.

"My god, I see him!" he cried in delight. "He's running across the fields towards what looks to be a town."

"Does he have the picture?" Flora demanded, leaping up beside him and resting her foot on the steering wheel for balance as she tried to spot the German amongst the long grass.

"It's either the painting of your father, or a very unusual hat," Teddy concluded. "He's definitely holding something square above his head. Very awkwardly too, I might add."

"One of his arms is most likely in a sling," Flora reminded him. "I'm *so* glad I shot him when I had the chance."

"Come along, then!" Alice exclaimed, dragging Teddy down from the car and flinging her very fetching scarf across her shoulders in preparation for the cross-country dash, "let's follow him!"

"Shouldn't we take the car?" Teddy asked, rather bemused, looking longingly back at his Beauford.

"Not unless the suspension can handle a bit of off-road driving," Alice called out, already charging off into the fields. "The road goes in quite the opposite direction, Teddy – and besides, I'm sure the three of us can catch a man with a bullet in his arm and a painting on his head."

Alice made an excellent point, and Flora and Teddy immediately bounded after her. Alice, like Flora, was wearing a pair of slacks, a knitted sweater and flat shoes - much to her relief. Unlike Flora she was also sporting an extremely fetching burgundy beret, which she was forced to clutch to her head as she ran towards the Hungarian town in the middle-distance.

"I say, give it to me, Ali," Teddy shouted as he saw her effort to retain her headgear. "I'll tuck it in my pocket."

"Thank you, darling, but you'd only squash it. Do you remember when you looked after that charming little boater for me for an afternoon last summer? Disaster – I've had to give it to ma to add to the dogs' dressing up box."

Alice's mother – enthusiastic chairwoman of her local Women's Institute – had taken to photographing her spaniels dressed as various whimsical human characters, in order to raise money for a number of worthy causes. "Pup goes Punting" had been a particular favourite at the WI Christmas Fair, and had made almost ten pounds for the campaign to renovate the local cricket pavilion.

Flora grinned at this exchange as she steamed past Alice, displaying the kind of speed which had made her much sought after by St. Penrith's hockey team. Alas, she had always resolutely refused every invitation to join their number, considering, as she did, that outdoor matches held in the depths of winter in nothing but a small maroon skirt and cotton shirt were the height of insanity. On a Saturday afternoon she was far more likely to be discovered tucked in a corner with a novel in one hand and a gin and tonic (masquerading as lemon squash) in the other. Alice had tried her hand at hockey on only one occasion, and had attracted a lifetime ban when it became clear that her anarchic sensibilities extended to more than just politics. Nobody disputed the fact that the vile girl from Cheltenham Ladies College who'd deliberately tripped Alice deserved a sharp, unobtrusive rap on the shins - it was generally considered, however, that wresting the hockey stick from her opponent's hands, giving forth to a blood-curdling war-cry, and charging after her swinging the stick around her head like a mace, had perhaps been a slight over-reaction.

The three friends had covered a fair amount of ground, although without the vantage point offered by the front seat of the Buick it was difficult to make out how much distance still lay between them and the German. A church spire was visible not too far ahead, however, and Teddy reckoned that it was probably now less than a mile to the outskirts of town.

Just as he was informing his companions of this fact, the sound of an engine filled the sky above their heads: Alice very nearly threw herself to the ground, fearing that the German had somehow procured air support. Pausing for a moment, Flora pushed the hair from her eyes and looked up. "Bertie?" she cried out in surprise, shouting so that her companions might hear her over the din. "I'm fairly sure that's the Cynthia-Rose!"

It certainly looked like Bertie's plane; the yellow paint shone like gold in the afternoon light, and hints of a cursive script were visible on its flank as it swooped above them. The three figures below waved as vigorously as they could, trying to attract the pilot's attention. Whether they were successful or not remained a mystery, however, as the plane continued on its way and seemed to sink to the ground close to the town.

"How could he know where we are?" Teddy asked, much impressed and swiftly calculating how he might be able to upgrade the Beauford to something of a more aeronautical flavour.

"Do you think he saw us?" Alice asked, still determinedly clutching the beret to her auburn hair and looking up at the trail of smoke the plane had left through the cloudless sky.

"It may be that Magda managed to get through to London," Flora postulated as she continued to yomp towards the town with a renewed purpose. "Although I don't know how they'd have got hold of him in Austria, since we have his radio."

"I must say, Flor," Teddy said, seizing Alice by the hand and running after her, "that you really do have the most extraordinary family. Fancy your uncle being a spy for the British government – and the key to the whole thing being your mother's portrait of your father!"

"Well, Ted," Flora replied grimly, "it won't mean a thing unless we collar that German in time. I *cannot* fail them now."

Once again the three friends felt the eyes of future generations upon at them, willing them to succeed. It was in silence, then, that they resumed running the final kilometre towards their destination.

NINE

Neither Flora nor Teddy nor Alice knew quite what they'd expected to find when they arrived in this new town, set against the rolling green hills and dense woodland; perhaps a sleepier version of Szentendre, a rural Hungarian idyll populated by farmers and labourers, with a quiet market square and an ancient church. As it was, they arrived to find something quite, quite different. The old church was there, certainly, and the first people they encountered were indeed wearing smocks and clogs and blessed with the kinds of sunburnt faces which spoke so eloquently of a life spent outdoors. The dying afternoon sun bathed the cobbled streets in a gentle glow, and the buildings were painted in variously faded shades of apricot. There was even a goat meandering across the road in front of them, a piece of straw caught between his lips and a bell hanging from its scrawny neck. There, however, the similarities ended. For in addition to the Hungarian versions of Seths or Reubens which the three had foreseen, the town also appeared to be full to the brim with young bohemians. The closer they got to the centre of town the more hectic it became, until eventually Alice declared that it felt decidedly like May Morning in Oxford.

And indeed, it did have something approaching that feeling of madness. Young people in louche clothing were bellowing at one another good naturedly, a fog of cigarette smoke hanging above them and bottles of wine being passed around. The sound of a jazz band was emanating from one of the many heaving cafés, and Teddy very nearly got into an altercation with a particularly tipsy young man who seized Alice around the waist before kissing her roundly on the mouth –the only thing that saved the fellow from ending up on the ground was that he was wearing lipstick and some kind of Renaissance cap, which made the fundamentally conservative Teddy Fortesque feel wildly uncomfortable.

Most surprising of all, however, was the fact that the town was brimming with artists. Tortured looking men were dashing about with paintings clutched to their chests; framers stood on street corners trying to sell their wares; and excited enthusiasts drifted from stall to stall, wondering which piece deserved their hard earned money. An intricately painted sign hanging above the fountain in the middle of the town square declared this to be the Pilisszentkereszt Air Fair; Flora translated for her friends.

"For heaven's sake," Alice howled in frustration, stamping her foot on the cobbled street, "of all the days to run in to a pack of ruddy artists. Just look at them all, Flor – how are we ever going to find the German amongst this lot?"

The challenge was clear. The square was literally awash with men in dark clothing, paintings tucked under their arms and dark hats casting shadows across their faces. They moved en masse, like a single organism, urgently seeking the next Magritte. A lone figure with an immeasurably valuable frame wouldn't be easy to find – it would either be a case of blind luck or extreme cunning.

A passing young lady daubed in dramatic make-up handed a bottle of schnapps to Teddy, and before he had time to think he'd instinctively imbibed a healthy mouthful. "Thanks awfully," he said, returning the bottle to its exotic owner with a grin.

"Teddy," Flora said severely, "there will be plenty of time for drinking afterwards. Now let me sit on your shoulders so I can have a proper look around."

Teddy obediently fell to his knees and gathered his friend onto his shoulders. He stood slowly, holding Flora by the ankles. Taking a moment to steady himself and with assistance from Alice, he hoisted himself up onto the fountain's stone surround in order to give them a better view. Alice leapt up next to him so that she too could scan the crowds.

"Do you see anything?" Teddy called up to Flora, gradually turning in a circle.

"Not yet," she replied, holding her hand over her eyes to shield them from the light of the dying sun. "Keep turning, Ted."

Alice held her breath and willed the German into sight, itching to confront him for what he'd done to her friend. The band suddenly struck up a fast gypsy swing number and the crowd began to pulse quickly in time to the music, parting like blades of grass caught in a breeze before springing back together on the next beat. It was during one of these sweaty partitions that Flora caught a glimpse of a single figure standing rigidly on the other side of the square, his face a picture of disgust.

"Got him," she cried, before scrambling down from Teddy's shoulders. "Follow me!"

"I say, Flor," Teddy shouted after her, "what if he's armed?"

His voice was drowned out by the roar of the crowd, however, and Flora was already slipping through the bodies after her target. Of course, she thought to herself as she fought her way towards him – a true Nazi would never be able to enjoy Romani music. Suddenly, just as she arrived in the middle of the square and to her horrified surprise, Flora found herself lifted from the ground, arms pinioned to her sides.

"*Teddy!*" she shouted, before a giant hand clamped across her mouth. And then, for the second time that day, the world went dark.

Flora felt herself being flung over her captor's shoulder and carried into a building before being dumped unceremoniously into a chair. Her ankles were roughly bound to the legs of her seat, and her hands were fixed tightly behind her back. The cloth covering her head was removed, and Flora blinked rapidly as her eyes readjusted to the light. She saw Alice had also been gagged and trussed up next to her, her green eyes staring at Flora in panic. Teddy was lying unconscious in the corner of the deserted café – evidently, he'd given their kidnappers rather more trouble. A nervous looking waiter responded to a command issued in curt German, and scuttled across to the door, putting the "closed" sign in the window.

"*So*," a German voice said. Flora's nemesis slithered out of the shadows from the back of the room, cupping his injured arm with his left hand. "You have led us on quite the wild duck chase, Anasztázia."

Alice snorted in spite of herself, and rolled her eyes at Flora. The German scowled at her.

"Silence!" he said. "Or would you like to join your friend here in sub-consciousness?" He pointed at Teddy and narrowed his eyes.

Two extremely large Aryan men suddenly walked out of the store-room at the back of the café, pushed the petrified looking waiter to one side, and joined the German in front of Flora.

"We must stop meeting like this," Flora said conversationally, looking up at those welted cheeks. "Given that you seem to insist upon it, however, might I at least have the pleasure of your name?"

"My name?" the German repeated, eyebrows raised in hauteur. "I see no harm in that. I am Förster."

"Förster?" Flora repeated.

"Yes, Förster. Like your writer, you know – *A Room with a Ewe*."

"Nearly," Flora said, smiling sweetly.

"We are not here to discuss literature," Förster said tartly. "Your uncle was a traitor to the Fatherland. Naturally, he had to die." Förster stroked his arm as he spoke, and paced slowly back and forth in front of his captives.

"Then he gave his life for an excellent cause," Flora said simply. "No true Hungarian could ever believe the evil your party peddles. And neither could any Briton."

Alice stamped her bound feet in agreement and nodded vigorously.

"I said be quiet," Förster spat, turning on his heel before hitting Alice hard across her face.

The last time Flora had encountered the German, it had been a very dark night. Under the harsh lamp light of the café, however, his white duelling scars gave his angular cheeks a cruel sharpness, and his small, black eyes stared out of their deep sockets with a burning intensity. Unlike his vast companions, Förster was dark and lean. The wounded arm sitting in a sling gave his bony body yet another plane; with his free hand he placed a cigarette between his teeth and lit a match.

"Your uncle," he said, exhaling a cloud of smoke, "was executed before this list of his made its way back to England - which means that you are the only other person to have seen it, Anasztázia."

"Miss Medveczky, please," she replied smoothly.

The German gave a sharp laugh. "As you wish," he said with an ironical bow.

"I must say," Flora observed, somehow managing to look almost nonchalant in spite of her extremely precarious situation, "that I hadn't given a great deal of thought to this new German regime of yours before now. Your ravings are obviously well reported in the British press, but *really*. *Mein Kampf*? It's hardly Tolstoy, is it? I owe my uncle a great debt, really. I shall certainly think twice before holidaying in the Bavarian Alps again, let's put it that way."

Förster sneered and leant over her, plucking the cigarette from his lips and holding the burning embers uncomfortably close to Flora's right eye. "There shall be no more holidays for you, young lady. It is a shame you have to die - you certainly have…sprite."

"I think you mean spirit," Flora replied coldly. "And I'm afraid that there will be no dying today. We both know it would create a serious diplomatic incident if two innocent schoolgirls and Varsity's most promising young spin bowler were to be discovered murdered in a Hungarian village. My housekeeper has already alerted London to my whereabouts and your involvement, so there could be no doubt as to the perpetrator."

From the corner of her eye, Flora noticed that Teddy had begun to stir. Determined to keep Förster occupied, she suddenly changed tack, leaning back in her chair and smiling up at him. "I knew a boy called Forster once," she said with a small shake of the head. "A grotty little zit from St. Penrith's for Boys. He used to shoot at songbirds with an air-rifle from his dormitory window, as I recall. Didn't he, Alice?"

Alice nodded, and even managed a smirk.

"He was expelled, in the end: something to do with attempting to throttle his house-master's spaniel. I wonder if he was a relation? The similarities are pronounced."

Peeling the glove from his left hand with his teeth, Förster suddenly stepped towards Flora and slapped her firmly across the cheek. "I have had enough of your imprudence," he growled.

"Impudence, I think," Flora muttered under her breath, refusing to react to the stinging blow.

Spitting the cigarette from his lips, Förster reached for the gun at his hip. Taking that as his cue, Teddy sprang up from the ground like a wild cat and seized one of the enormous German soldiers from behind. "Don't move," he said in a low voice, wrapping his muscular forearm around the German's neck, "or Claus here gets it."

The second German henchman snarled, drew a gun from the depths of his leather jacket, and pointed the weapon at Teddy. Teddy simply tightened his grip around his hostage's neck and manoeuvred himself behind the man's body, using him as a human shield. The soldier's eyes bulged with pain and panic, and he urged his friend not to shoot in a choking voice. "I could break his neck in an instant," Teddy promised the room, tightening his grip still further. "These arms of mine are the reason I'm known as the Harold Larwood of Oxford's first eleven." This obscure cricketing reference was entirely lost on the Germans in the room, but Flora and Alice both nodded in full agreement.

"He really is exceptionally strong," Alice confirmed, having managed to work the gag out of her mouth. "I once watched him beat a circus strong-man in an arm wrestle at the Eagle and Child – he was *magnificent*."

"Thank you, darling," Teddy replied, much moved by this tribute.

Without saying anything, Förster drew his own weapon and pointed it at Alice's forehead. "Let him go, young man," he said with mounting irritation. He cocked his gun. "Unlike your friend here, I don't miss."

"Don't pay any attention to him, Teddy," Alice declared, staring down the barrel of the gun without displaying the slightest flicker of fear. "Just keep hold of that fascist lump."

The muscles of Teddy's forearm twitched, and he looked across at Alice in despair.

"My god, this is absurd," Flora cried, infuriated that her friends should suddenly find themselves in danger. "You've got the list, Förster – Alice and Teddy haven't even seen it. Just let them go."

"You should do as the girl says, you know," a male voice observed from the back of the room. Everybody snapped their heads around in unison.

The waiter, who had previously seemed so cowed by fear, was now leaning casually against the café's bar, holding a cigarette and glass of red wine in one hand, and a pistol in the other. He had appeared rather small before, scurrying out of the way of the Germans, but now Flora realised that he must have been well over six foot. The apron had been removed to reveal a finely tailored suit, the man's face was extremely handsome in a vulpine sort of a way, and a wave of black hair fell across his forehead. He had spoken in impeccable English, but Flora could hear the trace of Hungarian in voice.

"Crikey," she said under her breath, looking at this new player in fascination.

"Do you know him, Flor?" Alice whispered, fixing her eyes on the extremely dapper gentleman, who was in turn surveying the trio of Germans with cool loathing.

"We've never met," Flora replied, "but I think that may be my uncle."

"Hans," Förster said in his clipped voice, addressing his last available lackey in German, "shoot Miss Medveczky."

It seemed to Flora that the next minute unfurled itself in slow motion. Seeing Hans raise his gun, she seized Alice by the hand and threw her weight backwards, tipping their chairs so that their feet flew up into the air and their bodies hurtled towards the hard floor. Just before she and Alice hit the stone, Flora saw another male figure leap through the open window of the café and roll across the ground, a gun in his hand. Three guns were fired almost simultaneously, and Flora felt the air knocked from her lungs. Her right foot was twisted by an unknown force as it hung suspended in the air. And then there was silence.

"Flora!"

"Bertie?" she asked, trying to catch her breath as her eyes focused on the swinging lamp in the centre of the white ceiling. "Is that you?"

"Yes, it's me, alright," he confirmed, falling to his knees and looking into her face for signs of injury or concussion. "Are you hurt?"

"Nothing but a few bruises," she said, twisting around to check that Alice was unharmed. "All alright, Ali?"

"Absolutely fine, my love," Alice replied cheerfully, rubbing her hands as Teddy untied her from the chair.

As Bertie peeled her from the floor and helped her onto her feet, Flora saw that the mysterious Hungarian was standing in front of her, staring at her face. The unimpeachable suaveness which had characterised the man during his encounter with the Germans had been tempered by a look of almost awkward anxiety – and the blue eyes which had seemed so hard were now full of concern. He was indeed remarkably handsome, but now looked rather more like a charismatic don than a cold-hearted spy.

"Hallo, Uncle Antal," Flora said in Hungarian, laughing and offering a hand.

"Hello, Ana," Antal said with a relieved smile, throwing his half-smoked cigarette to the ground before drawing her into a hug.

As her head rested on her uncle's shoulder, Flora noticed two things: first, that one of the Germans had apparently managed to shoot the heel from her very smart shoe; and secondly that Förster and his two minions were lying dead on the ground. "What happened?" she asked, taking a step back and looking at the three men standing before her.

Antal, Bertie and Teddy exchanged glances, and very politely waited for one of the others to explain.

"Do go ahead, sir," Teddy said, looking at Antal. "After pulling off that top-notch disguise, you deserve the honours. Although, I must say that your front roll through the window was also *extremely* impressive," Teddy added, turning to Bertie.

"You're too kind," Bertie said, with a twitch of the lip. "After you, Mr Medveczky."

"Thank you gentlemen," Antal said graciously, responding to the glint in Bertie's eye with a smile of his own. "Well then - seconds after you and your friend threw yourselves backwards, Ana – and that was very quick thinking, by the way, well done you – Förster's bullet caught your shoe, and mine found his heart. This young gentleman –whom I assume is my contact from the Agency?" Bertie nodded. "Well, his timing couldn't have been better, I'm happy to say, and he managed to disarm Hans here before he could fire at your friend. And as for Claus...."

"Yes...I can fill you in on that, if you like, sir," Teddy replied with a rather rueful grin. "I'm afraid that I rather forgot myself in the heat of it all, and entirely cut off the poor chap's air supply. He'd been limp for at least two or three minutes by the time you arrived," he said, looking to Bertie. "I didn't want to give the game away, of course, as his death would rather have taken the sting out of my threat to kill him, so I just sort of....propped him in place, if you know what I mean. In fact the heel of your shoe hit him on the forehead, Flor," he added, "so in the end I was jolly glad to have kept him there. It looked to be extremely painful."

"Might I ask," Bertie said, looking a touch nervously around the café, "where the painting is, Mr Medveczky? Do you have it safe?"

"After a fashion," Antal replied, quite cheerfully. "Now, I suggest that we get out of here before the police arrive. I know an excellent restaurant on the other side of town, and the proprietor is a friend. We shall be quite safe there."

TEN

Before many minutes had passed, the group were gathered around a long wooden table in a dimly lit restaurant, drinking pálinka and eating sausage casserole. Teddy had flung a protective arm around Alice the moment they had left the café and had refused to move it since, and Bertie, who was sitting next to Flora, kept looking at her out of the corner of his eye, checking for as yet undiscovered injuries. She took this in remarkable good grace, but refused to be fussed over. Antal sat at the head of the table, his long legs stretched out in front of him as he smoked a cigar, looking at the people sitting before him with admiration.

"My God, Ana," Antal said, leaning forward to take his niece's hand. "I needed someone I trusted to keep an eye on the painting until I could get it to London, but I never thought you would be in any danger." He shook his head in dismay. "I suspected that my cover was under threat, but until I was given that final name in Paris I never imagined that the Germans would head to the castle, or embroil you in this – for all they knew, the list was with me. When I realised that I'd led you straight into harm's way...."

"It's quite alright, really," Flora said, squeezing her uncle's hand, "I was only loafing about at school, and

I'm *so* pleased you entrusted me with it. The final name, though," Flora asked, a wrinkle appearing on her clear forehead, "what do you mean? What does the list have to do with it?"

Uncle Antal released his niece's hand, and sat back in his chair, tapping his cigar against the side of the ashtray. "You have a Miss Baxter teaching at your school?"

Alice and Flora both nodded slowly.

Antal put the cigar back between his lips and in a cloud of smoke, declared, "Hers was the last name."

Alice gasped, Flora swore in Hungarian, and Teddy's eyes boggled.

"Indeed. According to my French contact Miss Baxter's fiancé was killed at the Somme, sending her quite mad with grief. She blamed the British government for her loss and in the early 20's became associated with a small group of foreign nationals hell bent on bringing England to its knees.

Eventually the Nazi party got wind of this faction – the Crimson Tide, they call themselves – and Miss Honoria Baxter was recruited to Hitler's cause. She's been operating under a number of different code names, and working in Westminster as a secretary during the school holidays – enabling her to feed information back to Berlin, whilst maintaining her cover as a respectable Housemistress at your school."

"Miss Baxter was with me when I received your telegram," Flora said, blanching slightly. "She only joined the School last year, so it makes sense. No wonder Förster was on to us so quickly, Bertie."

"Well," Alice said in a state of advanced indignation. "The *number* of times I said there was something fundamentally wrong with that woman. I do wish parents were more receptive when one tells them that one's Housemistress is unbalanced - it's all very well saying that every child thinks their teachers are vile, but when one of them actually forces fourth formers to recite Thus Spoke Zarathustra during the inter-house singing competition, when everyone else is doing Gershwin..."

Flora helped herself to one of Bertie's cigarettes. "It certainly explains a great deal," she observed, maintaining an admirable degree of calm.

"She's a bally lunatic," Teddy added, eying the bottle of pálinka with some interest. "Do you know that she took a pot-shot at Guss Fenton-Digby when she found him clambering over the Girls' School wall after a nocturnal visit to his young lady? Very nearly put a bullet in his backside the day before he was due to lead the first eleven out against Marlborough. Quite mad."

"Well, this should draw her reign of terror to an end," Bertie observed. "And what about you, sir?" he asked, handing the bottle to Teddy and looking across at Antal, "How did you end up here? Flora was quite convinced that you were dead."

"Your telegram definitely used the word "curtains,"" Flora confirmed, raising the glass to her lips and thoughtfully appraising her uncle.

"Yes, well it very nearly was," Antal said frankly. He rested his cigar in the ash-tray next to his arm, and leant back in his chair. "It began about a month ago, just after I'd made contact with London to let them know that I was coming in. The list was almost complete, you see, but as soon as I made that call I suspected something was wrong; an instinct, honed over the years..."

"We're investigating the possibility of an internal leak, sir," Bertie said gravely. "I fear someone in my office destroyed your cover."

"It wouldn't surprise me in the least if that turned out to be the case," Antal replied calmly. "I've heard whisperings of something of the sort going on in London for months. Your employers need to handle that particular issue before anyone gets hurt. As it was, I managed to contain the problem."

"So why the message to me?" Flora asked. "If you knew the game was up, why send it?"

"Because there was one last name to secure before I could deliver the list, Ana," he replied. "And the last person I thought they'd be on to was a schoolgirl.

I knew I had to get to Paris to meet the person I hoped would be able to give me the final piece to the puzzle. I also knew that there was a jolly good chance that Förster's men would find me before I made contact with my informant, so I left a draft of my telegram at the hotel and told them to send it to you if I hadn't returned by six o'clock the following morning. As it was, I was able to get the information I needed just in time, and before the Germans opened fire. I was not, however, in a position to halt the telegram."

"What happened, sir?" Teddy asked.

Again Uncle Antal put the cigar between his lips, his words carried forth on a wave of smoke. "My contact and I met at Notre Dame, as planned. Just as she was giving me Miss Baxter's name, two men emerged from the shadows and opened fire. My contact was killed instantly, and I flung myself backwards into the Seine, as though I had too been shot. It was so damnably cold in that river that I very nearly froze to death – however, I was able to climb out unseen on the opposite bank, and managed to track the two Germans back to their own hotel."

Uncle Antal paused as the waiter carried another bottle of palinka to the table, and waited until everyone had a full glass. "I spent the next few days trailing the Germans," he continued, "to try to ascertain their next move. I was posing as a waiter at a café on the Champs-Élysées the day before yesterday when I overheard them discussing Miss Baxter. They were laughing about the fact that I'd died before joining the dots – in other words, before I had had a chance to discover that one of their moles was a Housemistress at your school, Anasztázia; no doubt put in post to keep an eye on you, in case I ever made contact. My God, when I realised that there was a chance Baxter could have intercepted my telegram...."

Uncle Antal's eyes grew dark at the memory, and his fingers curled around the glass in his hand.

"There was absolutely nothing you could do," Flora pointed out to him. "Miss Baxter really is a pill."

Antal looked at her and smiled slightly. "I can quite imagine. Your father and I were both plagued by a particularly unpleasant teacher at school – and not even he turned out to be a fascist spy. As far as I know, of course."

"And how did you end up here, sir?" Teddy asked. "Did you know Flora would be at the castle?"

"I hoped she would," he replied. "My options, you see, were sadly limited - if I tried to make contact with London to ask them to protect Anasztazia then I risked revealing my position and hers to the double-agent within your agency, Bertie. I therefore concluded that the most effective solution would be to continue to shadow the Germans, find out what they knew, and, as it turned out, follow them to Hungary."

"In the meantime, of course," Bertie interjected, "I had found Flora, and brought her to Szentendre in the Cynthia-Rose. Where Förster was waiting for us."

"Baxter must have put him on the scent," Alice interjected. "*Fiend.*"

"Which means I did put you into danger as soon as I sent that damned message," Antal said bitterly. "What a fool."

"It was really the Germans who were in danger," Bertie said, smiling broadly. "Flora shot Förster during our first encounter with him, sir – she kept her head throughout all of it, and never once showed a hint of fear. Of course I tried to run resistance, to keep her as safe as possible. Which seemed to work rather well, until I was called away to Austria." Bertie looked murderously down at the sausage casserole.

"You weren't away very long, Bertie," Flora observed. "What was it all about?"

"Absolutely nothing, I'm afraid," he replied after a moment. "Bad information - no doubt intended to get me out of the way long enough to enable Förster to get his hands on that painting. I distrusted the tip-off at once, of course, but if I hadn't gone then I would have been disobeying a direct order and risking ejection from the agency."

"I think it'd be best if you didn't radio in to your team for a little while," Antal observed. "At least until we get the painting safely to London."

"I agree," Bertie replied, nodding slowly. "I've already disabled the radio on the Cynthia-Rose, and intend to stay dark until this is over."

"I still don't understand how you ended up in the café, sir," Teddy asked. "How did you know that that's where Flora would be?"

"I didn't," Antal replied, grimacing slightly. "But I knew that that was the agreed rendezvous for the Germans – and that if they managed to get the painting away from Flora, this is where they would be heading. It was an impossible decision, Ana," he said, looking over at his niece. "I couldn't bear the idea of anything happening to you, but neither could I let that painting get back to Germany."

"Really, there's no need to explain," Flora replied. "I just feel awful that I let Förster take the painting from me." She tried a small smile. "Rather a poor show from me in the end, as it turns out."

"Ana," Antal cried, taking her by the hand, "if it hadn't been for you and your friends, Förster would have taken that painting to Berlin days ago. What you did brought us precious time – I never expected you to protect it indefinitely. Just long enough to give me a chance to find a solution. And now," he added, "I have it safe."

"What!" Alice cried. "We didn't see it in the café – I assumed Förster had managed to palm it off on one of his lackeys!"

"Precisely, my dear," Antal replied. "As far as Förster was concerned, he handed the frame over to one Lieutenant Gruber." There was the sound of clattering on the stone stairs. "I imagine this is him now."

A German officer suddenly burst into the room, the painting clutched to his chest.

"Don't shoot!" Antal commanded, as Bertie raised his pistol and Teddy seized the silver salt- cellar in front of him, determined to put his bowling prowess to good use.

"You must leave immediately," the man said in Hungarian, pressing the painting into Antal's hands and moving swiftly to the back of the room. "German support has arrived, and they're tearing the town apart in search of you." As he spoke, the young man disappeared behind a mountain of vegetables and flung open a small, dark door concealed in the wall.

"This is Péter," Antal explained, walking quickly towards the hidden passage-way. "He's been posing as a German soldier for the past year."

If Flora, Bertie, Alice and Teddy were surprised, they didn't show it. Instead they rose from their seats, and quickly following Antal's lead.

"The passage passes through the cellars, under the streets," Péter explained. "It will take you to Imre's shop on the edge of town, and from there you can make your way across the fields. Go, quickly."

"Thank you, my friend," Antal said, shaking Péter's hand before plunging into the darkness. Bertie plucked a torch from his pocket and handed it to Flora, who took Alice's hand and followed her uncle. Teddy brought up the rear, still clutching the salt- cellar and wearing a grim expression. Péter closed the door behind them - apart from the ray of light emanating from the torch, they were now in total darkness.

The group made their way silently through the dank passage-way, trying to ignore the sound of scuttling rodents and the bone-chilling coldness of the wet stone walls.

"Anasztázia," Antal said quietly, "when we reach the end of the passage, you go with Bertie. I need the pair of you to get that frame to London."

"The Cynthia-Rose isn't far, sir," Bertie said. "I give you my word that I'll get Flora home safely."

"What about you," Flora asked, raising her hand in the half-light to rest it on her uncle's shoulder, "where will you go?"

"My car is just across the fields, sir," Teddy interjected. "There'd be plenty of room, if we could be of any assistance?"

"Yes, *do* come with us," Alice added, very taken with the idea of helping her friend's extraordinary relation escape the Germans. "The car is positively laden with wine, and we'd be more than happy to take you anywhere you might want to go."

"You are both very kind," Antal replied, permitting himself a brief laugh, "and I must say that your offer is a welcome one. Were you intending to head back to England?"

"I have a spot of business in Burgundy, sir – I've promised to pick up a case or two of vino for a chum back in Oxford, you see – but yes, after that we intend to venture back across the Channel. Alice should be back at school before too long, and I've got Collections to think about." Teddy blanched – in the face of Nazi hostility he had remained resolutely courageous, however the thought of his impending exams filled him with a sense of doom. Failure seemed imminent, and Pa Fortesque was unlikely to take it well.

"What are you reading?" Antal asked, just as a large rat ran across Flora's shoe, very nearly causing her to scream.

"Greats," Teddy replied with a shudder. "In retrospect, an extremely poor decision on my part. Translating "veni vidi vici" seems to be about all I can muster, and the less said about my Greek the better."

"It just so happens," Antal said, kicking a rat from his own shoe with the precision of a fly-half, "that I myself read Classics at Cambridge, many years ago. If you can get me safely to England, young man, I should be more than happy to tutor you for a few weeks."

"*Sir*," was all Teddy was able to offer in response, moved as he was by the enormous self-sacrifice of Antal's offer.

"We're nearing the end of the passage," Bertie said over his shoulder, as Flora shone the light on what appeared to be a heavy wooden door. "Quiet now."

Flora flicked off the torch as Bertie crept towards the door, straining to hear signs of movement on the other side. Satisfied by the echoing silence, he took the door's metal ring in his hand and twisted it slowly. The creaking of the hinges filled the air, and the group held their breath as Bertie eased the door open and moved forwards with his gun at the ready.

"All clear," he called back after a moment, and the rest of the collective moved out of the tunnel and into the shop's small storeroom. "We don't have much time, chaps – the Germans are sure to discover the tunnel before too long. Best say your goodbyes whilst I get my bearings." And with that he moved to the other end of the room, wiped the dust from the window-pane and stared intently at the horizon.

Antal and Flora looked at one another. "Not much time for a proper catch-up now, I fear," Flora said with a rueful smile. "And there's so much I should like to talk to you about."

"Your father would be very proud of you, Anasztázia," Antal replied, pulling his niece into a quick hug. "I promise I shall find you as soon as I'm in England."

"Please do," she said, smiling through her sudden tears, before taking the painting from him and tucking it under her arm. "You must come to tea – I'm sure mama would be delighted to see you again."

"Right," Bertie said in his efficient way, signalling to Teddy to come to the window. "The road to Szentendre is thirty degrees in that direction, so I imagine your vehicle must be a mile or so across those fields."

"That's right," Teddy said, scrutinising the scene and nodding in agreement. "She's just out of sight, behind that dip."

"Jolly good," Bertie replied, offering his hand to Teddy. "The Cynthia-Rose is forty-five degrees that way, so this is it."

"Pip," Alice said with a broad grin. "I thought I might have a small party at Ma and Pa's for New Year's – you must come with Flors, Bertie."

"Delighted," Bertie replied, as Flora gave her friend a meaningful glare. "Until then." Turning to Antal, he saluted and said, "Get in touch once you're back in England, sir. I'll do my best to get to the bottom of the leak, and let you know when it's safe to come in. In the meantime, I'll make sure that the list ends up in the right hands."

Antal pushed open the side-door next to the window, looked up and down the small cobbled path for any

Germans, and nodded at Bertie. "I'll see you in London, then. Come along, you two." And with that Alice, and Teddy slipped out of the door and made off across the fields.

Bertie took the painting from Flora and smiled down at her. "Ready, Flors?" he asked.

"Lead the way," she replied, nodding briefly. With a deep breath and a quick backward glance, Flora followed Bertie out into the afternoon light.

ELEVEN

Four hours later the Cynthia-Rose glided across Wimbledon Common, landing effortlessly in the darkness. Flora, who had much missed Pongo's scarf on the return journey and was longing for a comb, gingerly ran her fingers through her knotted hair. She was, she realised, in urgent need of a gin and tonic.

"I wonder," Bertie asked, as he tucked the painting under his arm and helped Flora down from the air-craft, "whether you might like to join me for supper, Flora?"

She glanced up at him as her feet sought solid ground. "What date is it?"

"December 15th, I believe."

"I don't think I have any prior engagements," she said slowly, after a moment's contemplation. "So yes - that would be very nice, Freddie." Now that they were out of Hungary, and after some careful consideration during their journey home in the Cynthia-Rose, Flora had decided that the time had come to use Bertie's real name. She wasn't sure if she was quite ready to forgive him for his subterfuge, but neither was she willing to participate in a game of false identities. Pongo, Flora recalled with a frown, had once tried to maintain a second life in London to aid her fledgling career as an actress. It hadn't ended well – either for the fictitious "Tuppence Crawley", or for Pongo – particularly when Pongo's father had found himself watching "Tuppence" make her debut on the London stage in a decidedly racy adaptation of *The Duchess of Malfi*. "Oughtn't we deliver the painting to someone trustworthy in your mob first?"

"I don't think that's a good idea for the time being, Flors," Freddie said, throwing the cover over the Cynthia-Rose and guiding Flora towards his car. "I've made alternative arrangements."

"Oh?"

"I wonder," Freddie said thoughtfully, as he pulled a pair of cigarettes from his pocket, "have you ever been to Blenheim?"

Flora accepted one of the Austrian gaspers and looked up at Freddie with interest. "I haven't, I'm afraid. Although I hear Mr Churchill is absolutely charming."

"He is indeed," Freddie replied. "And he's invited us to dine with him this evening."

Flora paused for a moment, her eyes widening: the adventures of the past few days had not, apparently, entirely exhausted her capacity for surprise. Recovering her poise almost instantaneously, however, she moved towards the car and said over her shoulder, "I hope I'll have a chance to drag a comb through my hair before we head off for Oxford, Freddie. One doesn't want to appear vain, of course, but Mrs Churchill might not be terribly impressed if I arrived looking as though I had just emerged from a hedgerow."

"Hardly that," Freddie snorted, looking across at Flora who had, as far as he was concerned, maintained an untarnished glamour throughout their extraordinary time together. He jumped into the driving seat and, just before firing up the engine, turned to face her. "Before we go in search of a change of clothes and a hot bath, however...." Flora's heart lurched as Freddie gazed into her eyes. "Flora Mackintosh - I've been wanting to kiss you for days. Would you mind terribly if I did so now?"

Looking back at him, Flora realised that she was entirely amenable to being kissed by Freddie. Given how much they'd been through together, however, and knowing how fond she was of him, she decided to lay her proverbial cards on the table: no one would accuse Anasztázia Medveczky of being as cavalier with Freddie's heart as Antal had been with Anaïs', she thought to herself, sternly. "No, Freddie, I wouldn't mind at all."

"The *thing* is," she continued, stopping Freddie in his tracks and wishing she didn't look quite so dishevelled for this romantic denouement, "I intend to go to Cambridge next year, where I shall write what will be, for many, the seminal work on Henry James. I know of course that a kiss is just a kiss, but I certainly don't want to…well, to lead you on, Freddie."

Now, this was something of a first for Freddie. One wouldn't exactly call him a prolific kisser, but he'd had enough turns under the mistletoe to know that this was an unusual reaction. Rather than being deterred, however, this sudden declaration of independence only served to make him like her even more. "Flora," he said gravely, his eyes full of laughter, "I have no intention of putting a spanner in the works. If it would be helpful, however, I promise never to try to kiss you when you are in the throes of intellectual inspiration."

"Well then," Flora replied, greatly cheered by his understanding response, "as you were, Freddie."

THE END

Printed in Great Britain
by Amazon